Future Virtues

A Science Fiction Short Story Collection

S. A. Wooderson

Martin in the Woods Publishing

Book Cover by James Helps

Illustrations by Doli Young

For Katherina, my Muse

Chapter One

Till Death Do Us Part

Faith

FAITH

/fāTH/ noun

Believing in someone or something completely. Faith is by definition scientifically unprovable, and this unfounded belief system underlies all religions and cultures.

Contents

"Till death do us part," I said. And I meant it. Every word. Of course, I was 23 and I was immortal. We all are at 23. I was sure I was madly in love with him and together we would be happy. And I could say it was a good marriage, but what does that mean? It was an ok marriage. We had two kids, one son, one daughter, two jobs, ate meals together watching television, texted each other funny memes and occasionally laughed at the same jokes. We took vacations and celebrated all the things humans celebrate, all while buying each other useless things that neither of us needed. And then, when we were supposed to be winding down together, when the kids were just getting ready to leave the house, he died. And not in any kind of sudden, violent way that seemed like a cruel trick of fate. More in a quiet, sad, slow, painful way that colored everything that came before it. They call it cancer, and it is; it eats everything, and it ate Fred, and me too. At 46 I was a widow. And my daughter decided I needed to join a support group. You know, the kind of thing you see on TV, more a clique than a thing you think actually exists. And there I was, sitting in a room full of strangers who had all gone through what I'd gone through, all pretending we were there to process our grief but really just looking for people who hurt more than we did so we could feel better about our loss. That and look for someone to screw. Dating in your middle age is hard, and who better than someone else who was broken and shattered. Maybe together you could be whole.

Henry was a better husband than Fred. When we ate dinner the TV went off. He wanted to listen to me, to share with me. He appreciated me, appreciated all the things I did for him, and he was amazing in bed. And yet I knew Henry didn't love me the way he'd loved Sheryl, his first wife. He was just trying to replace her and I was a poor substitute. He would talk of her with such love in his eyes. Sheryl would sing while she did the dishes, she was the best cook, she had beautiful red hair. I really grew to hate Sheryl. I tried so hard to please Henry. It was never the easy companionship I had with Fred. But did I mention the sex was amazing? Henry was so fit and strong, he had such a great body, and he wanted me to join him at the gym. But I really couldn't do the 6 a.m. at the gym thing. It wasn't me. He would poke me in the soft places he said he loved as if he thought I was fat and ask me to go with him. He just wanted me to be healthy, he said. And when he dropped dead on the treadmill, before I cried—I couldn't help it—I started to laugh and didn't stop until I was rolling on the floor gasping and weeping. One massive coronary and at 50 I was a widow again. I was better at it the second time. I knew how to do grief and keep living. I knew that there were other people just as lonely as me. And I was not going to stay alone long.

My daughter and I went on a cruise. An expensive cruise bought with some of Henry's life insurance, and it was there that I met George. George was a widow with a navy pension and six different houses in San Diego he'd bought back when houses were cheap. George had started an electrical company and had been successful. Now at 60, he had just sold it and was retiring. The great tragedy in his life was that he and Mildred had never had children. I started to believe that my whole life had been leading to this. Being the third wife seemed to be the perfect job. Take the man who was retiring with lots of assets and no heirs and ride out the rest of my days in comfort. I wasn't madly in love with him the way I think I was with Fred, I wasn't sexually aroused like I was with Henry, but it was nice. I loved him. I was good at loving people, and I loved him enough. We ate good meals in good restaurants and traveled to places I had always wanted to go to. George wanted to make me happy like I had wanted to please Henry, and I was happy. We got married in Costa Rica on the beach and I felt free. That weight I had been carrying since Fred finally moved away and I didn't have to worry about paying the bills or looking after myself. George wanted to look after me. And it was nice. Until George drowned on a deep-sea fishing trip and I was left alone again, in a hotel in a foreign country. And I decided that was it. I had had enough. At 55 I was a widow for the third time. I had enough money that I never needed to work again. So I went back to our house in San Diego and did what lonely rich women do—I embraced the stereotype and had sex with the pool boy, and I felt worthless.

With a friend's help I dragged myself out of the house to the local homeless shelter and started volunteering. That was where I met Ernie. Ernie had lost his wife 5 years before. I attracted widowers. We shared the deep hurt that nothing would heal but that time turned into a low background noise, like muzak in the elevator. If you didn't pay attention to it you could pretend it wasn't there, and the minute you paid attention it was all you could think about.

Not sure what color to wear for my fourth wedding, I dressed in red and we got married at the courthouse, because I'd done every other kind of wedding I ever thought I wanted-ed. And the courthouse wedding was surprisingly lovely and touching. When the judge asked me if we would be married till death did us part, I felt my eyes welling up. It was a happy marriage. And we grew old together, until he died of everything we are supposed to die of—old age, in his bed, holding my hand. And it was sad but ok. I was ready to be alone.

The next two years I spent with my oldest daughter were so peaceful. I regretted not spending more years single.

My funeral was lovely. My daughter had become a born-again Christian somewhere between her youngest child becoming a teenager and her husband screwing a TikTok wannabe. So my funeral was conducted by her pastor. Pastor

Mike. I'd met him when I'd been living, gone to a few services—not my thing, but if it gave her solace, who was I to moan? I would like to blame Pastor Mike for everything that came afterward but it's probably bigger than him. Probably a large cosmic joke, like Donald Trump's hair and spray tan or everything tasting like chicken. You know, something that you just can't explain but is somehow vaguely funny.

She gave me a nice enough service. Lots of flowers, enough guests that the small room felt full. All my family were there, and Ernie's oldest daughter said really nice things about how happy I had made her father. Everyone seemed genuinely sad that I was gone. I never really thought that the dead could see their funeral but it made sense to me now how I had felt at all of my husbands' funerals. Of course, it was what Pastor Mike said that struck me most, especially afterwards. "God, we commit Gloria to your everlasting care. I know that you will welcome her into Heaven. Heaven waits for all of us, each of us in a large house given to us by God where we do not need to work, just live in peace with all those whom we love. For everyone we love is waiting for us up in Heaven, and there will live forever in his peace and his glory."

Actually, what struck me as Pastor Mike was talking was that his Heaven sounded a lot like the suburbs. Everyone in a large house, no one actually doing any work because the yard was mowed by Jose and the house cleaned by Maria. And I kind of wondered what kind of house Pastor Mike lived in, if maybe he was living in his car, and whether I should have given him more money when I was alive. Well, there was nothing I could do about it at that point. My daughter had inherited the house so if she wanted to buy Pastor Mike a nice condo before he got to Heaven and got that big Heaven suburb house, that was up to her. Then Pastor Mike started to sing, and play the ukulele. I kid you not, the ukulele. Obviously even the guitar was a little too expensive for his budget. I mean, I would have asked for organ music and a classically trained singer if I'd really given any thought to my funeral at all. But I had never planned to be there, and it was amusing, like being sent to the afterlife at a luau.

And that was how I arrived at the pearly gates, wiggling and trying to do the hand swishing thing I have seen so many times in Hawaii at the Cultural Center. The gates were open, and St. Peter was not there to greet me. So just in case you are looking for someone official, this was not like arriving to a government office. There was no one at the reception desk. There was no reception desk, just the vague idea of a pair of gates that perhaps my mind created and the very real presence of the people I loved, who were there to greet me.

My mom ran up and hugged me. My dad stood back waiting for my mom to finish. And then walking up George, and Henry, and Ernie and Fred, all of them looking younger than my memories of them, and hanging onto Henry was Sheryl; I recognized her from all the photos and recognized her horrible fake bottle-red hair. Her voice was a shocker. "Hen-ry," her shrill little nasal whine shot out across the area I realized now was a lawn in front of a large, beautiful house. The kind of house Pastor Mike had dreamed of, and it was lovely, classical French Provincial architecture but authentic looking, like that place George and I had rented that summer in Provence. And I realized that this was my ideal home and I wondered how the others saw it. "Henry, you belong to me, Henry," shrieked Sheryl, and I realized her ideal home probably looked a lot like a California modern McMansion, all white and glass with hard furniture and sharp angles. This was my Heaven. And everyone I loved was here. Everyone. My grandmama, who looked like she'd thrown on her clothes after a quick roll in the hay with my grandpapa, my Nana, who I hoped hadn't given up on baking now that she didn't have to work anymore, my Poppa, whom I recognized mostly from the belly he'd decided he still wanted to have, even in Heaven. And my mom and dad, and my sister Margarete, and my friend Rose, and worst of all George, Henry, Ernie and Fred. All of them, all together, all at once. Along with a first wife or two. And there in the corner, looking sheepish, were a couple of the guys I'd screwed in college. I mean, I thought I was in love but I was a kid then and damn, wow, they were dead. I'd never thought about that. In my memory they were still all 19.

So now here we are a month into Heaven. I have everything I ever wanted. I have everyone I ever loved and oh my God, I hate this place. I've slept with all my wasbands again and I have to say I really underrated Fred, and Pablo from College... ooh-la-la. This place is a regular French film but no one gets mad at each other. All of them have waited for me a long time, so I am disappointing them all. Of course, the other-wives club all hate me, and who am I to blame them. But everyone's so polite. All too scared to be anything other than perfect. Mildred says that if we are bad and argue we will go to Hell but I think she's an idiot. I sometimes also suspect that this might be Hell.

There doesn't seem to be anyone in charge, so I've started praying for the first time ever. I pretend that God looks like Pastor Mike with a ukulele and every day I ask if I can please leave Heaven and go back to Earth. My mom will miss me but she will understand, and I am hoping that maybe Fred will try to be reincarnated too. Maybe in our next life we could be Buddhists, be reincarnated as dolphins and avoid this whole Heaven thing altogether.

It would have to be better than Pastor Mike's Paradise.

Chapter Two

The Return of the Savior

The manicured blonde in the little heels leaned down to look at the boy. "Oh, how cute," she said, treating him like an inanimate object. She spoke of him not to him. "How old is he?"

"Three," said his mother.

"Oh, he's a cutie. What's his name?"

"Samuel."

She smiled. "Hi, Samuel."

"My name," responded the boy with a face as serious and passionate as a three-year-old's face could be, "is Jesus Christ."

"Samuel, stop that this instant. We've had this talk already..."

"Oh, how cute. He must have heard that in Church."

"We go to Synagogue."

"Oh." The blonde stood up and toddled away, not sure how to continue the conversation that was never meant to be anything more than a baby-fix moment for a woman who'd chosen a string of losers rather than a father type to be with.

Maya reached down and snatched up her child. "Samuel, don't do that."

"But Mommy, it's the truth."

"I don't know where you got this crazy idea from, Samuel. You are Samuel Liebowitz. I am your mom, Maya Leibowitz."

"But I said I'd return, Mommy. People need to know I'm back."

"You are never to speak of this again," she said in the worst voice he'd ever heard, worse even than that one she used when he drew on the wall with markers, worse than the one she'd used to talk to daddy last week. What was screwing around anyway? No one had explained it. He didn't really understand what was going on. What was everyone's problem? Weren't they expecting him? *It must be because I'm so small,* thought Jesus. *I'll grow and then I'll prove it to them.* "DO YOU UNDERSTAND?!"

"Yes, Mommy." He understood. He couldn't tell her the truth. He was an obedient child by nature. He didn't want to upset anyone. He would just keep quiet till they were ready. Till they were all ready.

****

He could hear them from his room but he tried to ignore them.

"What's he doing up there, Maya?"

"Reading the Bible again."

"I thought I told you to throw that damn thing out."

"I did. I think he stole the latest copy from a church; it's not my fault they're so easy to come by."

"It's just not normal for a nine-year-old boy. Can't you get him to go play football or something?"

"It's not like I haven't tried, Aaron. I ordered him to go to football and he did. He went there, stood on the field and refused to play. The coach asked me to take him home. There isn't a team in town that will take him now!"

"Goddamn it, Maya. We've got to do something; he's just not normal."

"The therapist says he'll grow out of it."

"The therapist's been saying that for two years."

Privately Jesus thought the therapist was coming around. He'd started to believe, to go to church again to re-embrace his faith. He had been hard work but Jesus needed disciples, and Paul the Therapist was the first.

He read through the signs of his coming again. What was wrong with these people? Didn't they see the signs? The earthquakes, the droughts, the famines, the wars, the hurricanes? I mean, it had all been translated so badly, and for that matter who had added all the schmaltz to what he'd said?

Wasn't there anyone capable of just taking notes and writing down something accurately? The amount of crap Peter had added to the Bible after he left was just appalling. If he ran into that guy again he'd have to give him a piece of his mind. Well, that would have to wait. He still needed to re-establish his position as the world's spiritual leader, and rule the world from his spiritual headquarters. And there was still study to do for tomorrow's spelling test, and that book report he had to write on *Charlie and the Chocolate Factory*. He hadn't finished reading the book yet. He'd better start. He didn't want to end up in detention at lunchtime; the cafeteria was serving hot dogs and he really liked them.

*   *   *

Jesus held the cat in his hand, its head to one side. Now to resurrect her again. She'd been harder to choke this time, probably because she'd wised up after the last time.

A scream cut the air and he looked up. "Samuel, oh my God, what have you done!"

He looked up. Why did she have such a strange look on her face?

"Nothing, Mom."

She ran and grabbed the cat from his hands and started to scream. She ran out of the room with the animal flopping in her arms.

She really should have left the cat with him; it'd be breathing again already. Oh well, the cat wasn't important. He was just practicing. He couldn't mess up when he showed the world his first miracle, and he was a little rusty.

Yeah, pretty soon he'd been on Oprah, raising the dead, then everyone would have to believe in him. Even Ellen DeGeneres would become a disciple, and he'd cure her. He rather fancied her, and now that he was fifteen it was time he had a harem. Fallen women had always been his favorite.

*   *   *

"What are you in for?"

"I'm Jesus."

"Nice to meet you. I'm Mohamed. Buddha and Confucius are standing over there." He pointed to the sofa where the three men sat staring at a television set with blank stares while white uniformed guards circled as if the drugged-up inmates would do anything.

"Oh, so how long do I have to stay?"

"They'll let you out after you stop saying who you are, or stop talking altogether. Between the shock treatment and the lobotomy, they're about ready to let Buddha go any day."

"But who's going to save the world?"

"Haven't you worked it out yet, kid? They don't want to be saved. They're fucked and there's not much we can do about it."

"So what do I do?"

"Take as many of the blue pills as you can get. They're a real fun ride."

Chapter Three

Karmic Redistribution

"**K** aar mik ree dist rra bu shon."

It took me a minute. Ah, Karmic Redistribution. I had finally reached them, and I'd only been on hold for twenty-nine hours. Twenty-nine hours of carrying my cell phone around with me. Twenty-nine hours of having the Bluetooth device in my ear listening for them to respond. Driving my kids home from school, only barely hearing them chatter, too busy listening to the muzak, waiting for it to change into a human voice. A whole night of not sleeping, only dozing as the drone of the muzak made me nod off, sucking down coffee to stay awake. But twenty-nine hours wasn't bad at all; I heard of one woman who rang the help line in 2004 because she thought Britney Spears had gotten her Karma. By the time she got through in 2007 to tell them this, she didn't really want to swap Karma with Britney, but it was too late to back out. Of course, I could hardly understand the operator through the thick Indian accent, but it wasn't that the office had been outsourced to India. Karma was an Indian concept and the offices had always been there. There was talk of moving their phone room to Ecuador, but the problem was how do you teach an Ecuadorian to speak English with an Indian accent?

"Ah, hello."

"Hello. Your name and Karmic number."

I looked down in the database, then shook my head. I wasn't doing this for a client; this was for me. "Megan Johnson, 5510294849 MJK 128g7y2349."

"Yes, Ms... Johnson. What can I help you with?" What kind of dumb question is that? I am calling Karmic Redistribution. Obviously I feel like I've been gypped, defrauded by this life; I deserve more and want it now. Now how to tone that down so I don't piss off the phone operator."Well, it's just that I've been working on my Karma..."

"We have a record of everything you've done. You can verify this on our website ."

"Well, yes, you have a record of everything but it's just that I don't feel like I'm getting my correct Karmic Credit."

"Do you believe someone else has your Karma?"

"No, well, not really. I mean I think I deserve better Karma. I'm a good person. I work hard, I look after my children, I just..."

"What is it that you want, Ms... Johnson?"

I should have been happy with this question. I mean, at least their operators were trained to listen and ask appropriate questions. It wasn't like calling the cell phone company. She even sounded like she might care, and since it was a 900 number and she was getting paid by the minute, goddamn, she could care. Goddamn it—was that what I was doing wrong? Had I pissed off some deity, was there one of them out there that still got pissed off if people took his name in vain? I mean, you'd think if you were God you could really get the hell over it by now— Oh, there I was, doing it again. Why was her question annoying me so much...

"Ms... Johnson?"

Ah, that was it. The name. I really should just change my name, get rid of the last vestiges of him for once and for all. But how could I? How could I ever be what I was before him? How could I change my name? It was the name of my children. I didn't want to have a name different from theirs, and I couldn't change their last name, their reality of who they were. It had been hard enough for them when we'd broken up, hard enough for them when he'd left, hard enough when he'd disappeared out of their lives, chasing some skirt in a different state. No, I couldn't disrupt their lives by changing my name now, but I didn't have to like it either.

"I want a better life."

"So there is someone you would like to swap Karmic Destiny with? Can I have the name of that person?"

I'd thought about this, a lot, even before I started the call twenty-nine hours ago, but there wasn't really any one person whose Karma I coveted. I mean, I could just jump out with an answer like "Oprah," but who knew if she really had what she wanted in life? I mean, she was immensely successful and rich but, was she satisfied or happy with her life? Was she loved? That's what I really wanted. I wanted to be loved. Really loved.

"There isn't anyone I want to swap Karmas with. I just have a question about my Karma."

"Have you filled out the appropriate online waivers concerning disclosing Karmic Potentials?"

"Of course I have." Why is it no matter how good of a mood you're in, when you finally get through to a call center they inevitably ask lots and lots of dumb questions that have you angry and riled up before you get off the phone? Of course I'd signed the disclosures and waivers. There had been at least 12 times I had had to confirm this, just like I'd had to key in my Karmic number and confirm my name, yet my name and Karmic number had been the first two questions.

"Alright, Ms... Johnson.""Call me Megan."

"Alright, Ms... Johnson. For insurance purposes I need to read the following statement to you. A third party will be listening in on the call to ensure quality control and accuracy. Is this acceptable to you?"Was saying no even an option? "Of course.""Ms... Johnson—""Megan."

"Alright, Ms... Megan Johnson, we have the third party on the line." It sounded slightly more echoey, like a heavy breather crank call but less committed. "I need your confirmation that you understand the possible outcomes of disclosures of Karmic Potential." She was sing-songing even more now that she had a memorized script to follow. I could understand the words but only just. "Karmic Potential is not necessarily an indicator of your life or success—that is still up to you. However, Karmic Potential indicates the most possible outcome of your current Karmic journey. Changes in the journey can occur without warning or reason, although self-generated change is the surest way to improve your Karmic outcomes. Any information we can give you on your Karmic Outlook can and should be seen only as a guide, and although we would like to present you with a positive Karmic outcome, we cannot guarantee to do so. Negative or positive Karmic Outlooks are only quantifiable for this time and place and we offer no guarantees or solutions. In fact the very act of hearing your Karmic Potential Outlook may by default change your Karma. Do you understand?"

"Yes." I get it. You tell me I'm going to be rich and I don't end up rich, I don't get to sue you to become rich. You tell me I'm going to die young and horribly, I don't get to go commit murder tomorrow. I don't get to use you guys as an alibi. Do I really want to know? Do I really want to know?

"Ms. Johnson, are you certain you would like a Karmic Potential Outlook?"

Do I really want to know? Will it change anything? Will I live my life differently if I know? Will I want to live at all? "Sure I'm certain."

"You understand that Karmic re-evaluation is a separate fee, and that you may at any time have your Karma re-evaluated for changes in your Karmic Outlook Potential?""Yes."

"You understand that you will only be allowed to ask one question for this Karmic Potential Outlook? Any further questions will have to be part of a new and separate call?"

"Yes."

"Did you get that?" She wasn't talking to me, just the heavy breather, and I heard him grunt and the echo disappeared off the line. "Ms... Johnson, is there a particular area you would like to know about?"

"Yes."She waited a second and I knew I had to say it, had to use the words.

"Love, my love life.""As I understand it, you would like to know the Karmic Potential Outlook of possible future love relationships?"

"Yes, I'd like to know if I'm going to find my soul mate, a man who will love me and whom I will love?"

"This is your question?""Yes, whether there is someone out there for me. Whether I will ever get married again..."

"One question only. I will consult the Karmic Wheel. Your question is will you find a man to love who loves you in return?"

"Yes."

"One moment, please." It was amazing, if you thought about it, that someone had managed to create the "wheel," which was a computer program, of course, not a real wheel, but it had been proven to be unerringly accurate, or at least as accurate as anything influenced by human behavior could be. If they hadn't invented the wheel they couldn't have begun to work on the Karmic redistribution engineering. The greatest use of the wheel had been back when it wasn't yet released for public consumption. The inventor, some computer geek whose name I couldn't remember, had taken it to all the world governments and shown them the future Karmic Potential of their countries. There'd been a lot fewer wars since then. What was his name again? I hated it when my brain didn't work, and that was what I should have asked about. I should have asked how long I was going to live, whether I would be healthy, something useful; instead all I cared about was whether or not anyone would ever love me.

"Ms... Johnson.""Yes.""The Karmic Potential of a positive response to your question is unlikely.""What do you mean?""It does not appear that you will have a man in your life who loves you and that you love. For the next five years it is definitely unlikely, for the five years after that it is fairly unlikely, and for the five years following that the chances increase, but only slightly. Further out than that the outcome is more vague, but not favorable for a positive response to your question."

I started to cry. I had told myself I wouldn't, at least not on the phone, not to a stranger, some woman in a sweatshop in India, but I couldn't help it. It wasn't fair, it just wasn't fair.

Other people could find love, other people had been in love more times than they could count, but I had never been in a relationship where I loved and was loved. *Why? Why me?* I wanted to scream at her. Instead all that came out was, "You mean there will be no love in my life?"

"Megan," she said, "there has always been love in your life, and there always will be. You are a very lucky woman."

"I don't understand."

"You love deeply, and are deeply loved in return."

I looked around the room. Trina had left her barbie on the sofa. Kerren's shoes were in front of the door where she had walked out of them. I bent to pick them up. "Megan, your life is filled with love," said the operator before switching back to her standard patter voice. "Thank you for calling Karmic Redistribution. We appreciate your business.""Thank you," I said, and she knew why I was thanking her. I hung up. I dried my eyes and cracked the door to my children's room. Trina had thrown all her covers off again. She slept naked, with one of her legs falling out of the bed. I walked over to her, put her leg back onto the bed and threw a cover over her loosely. Then I kissed her sticky forehead. Kerren was curled up in a ball, her teddy clutched to her, her face even in sleep serious and determined. I smoothed the worried lines off her forehead and kissed her cool velvet cheek.

Yes, there was love in my life. I let the warmth of the love fill me. She was right, I was very lucky.

Chapter Four

Waiting For My Number

I 've probably spent more hours playing bubble shooter on my phone than having sex.

This is the kind of thing that occurs to you during hour three at the DMV. The awareness that life is passing you by is all too evident in the glare of the florescent tubes. Looking at my watch for the seventieth time brought no relief. I was starting to question my own existence, and that was never healthy. They should probably have handed out Prozac at the door. I considered leaving. I should have left but they were only 10 people away from my number.

I found myself staring at the reflection of the room in the window. Maybe if I'd stared at the shiny-headed bald man it wouldn't have been different. Or I could have looked away in time, looked over again at the ball bearing piecing going through the back of the neck of the broad in front of me. But no, I stared at the window, my usual way of staring at people without staring at them. The guy behind me was going for another booger, certain no one was looking at him, while the blond woman next to him scratched at the roots of her extensions.

I wondered if anyone was staring at me, that middle-aged guy who is too tall and too fat to be comfortable anywhere, let alone the plastic chairs. He's pointing out into the aisleway so he's not squashing the bird next to him. He's so slouched all you can really see is the balding patch. Wondering how the world saw me made me straighten up a bit. Not as much as a real person because I'm pretty much a hunchback. Since reaching 6"4' at fourteen, I have always just kind of been ducking. Then the picture shifted. I blinked but the blond woman was definitely now a heavy black woman scratching at her dreadlocks, and the booger finder was a baby in a carrier.

And I was sitting on an old lady's lap. It was at about this point I fainted.

When I came to I was still at the DMV, lying on the floor, and the old lady was fanning me. "Damn it, honey, you're heavy."

"I'm sorry." How the hell did I end up sitting on this lady's lap? Shit, I could have done some serious damage.

"Oh, it's ok; you didn't know you was coming here. So how did you die?""Die?" Did she say die? Did the wrinkly old lady with the white cardie just asked me how I died? There was something a little off about her, obviously. She was smiling for starters. I mean, how many people smile at the DMV? And there was something else I couldn't quite pinpoint. Something different.

"Yes, honey, die. How'd you die?""I'm not dead. I was just sitting at the DMV and then, well..." I looked around. It looked like the DMV; there were still TVs hanging up with signs saying now serving D134. I looked down at the ticket in my hand. "Where's my ticket?" I said.

"You don't have a ticket yet. You only just got here."

I stood up, determined to get away from the crazy lady. I didn't know what was going on but if I was ever going to get the damn registration straightened out on that beater I had bought, I better get another ticket.

I picked myself off the linoleum tiles and walked towards the information booth in the center.

"Hi. Umm, I seem to have lost my ticket."

The woman at the information booth looked up. "Ok, sir. What is your name, sir?" She didn't look exactly like the woman I'd talked to earlier, but almost. She was middle aged, a little heavy, and had skin the color of gray coffee. I wasn't sure if the DMV only hired people who looked alike or whether years of working under fluorescent lighting made you look gray, heavy and old.

"Can I get the same number? I mean, I don't want to wait longer. I've already been waiting three hours."She glared up at me. "What's your name, sir?""I don't know what difference my name makes. I didn't give it to you last time. You just gave me a ticket."

"Sir, please give me your name."She was starting to get that "I am going to whoop ass on you" voice so I just thought it was easier to say it. "Charlie. Charles Wilson.""Ok." She looked down at a piece of paper that seemed to be changing as she looked at it. Sort of a weird shimmering, like words were just appearing and disappearing. Probably some new kind of tablet jerry-rigged to look like paper. "Yes, Mr... Wilson, died 1.49 p.m. at the Santa Clarita DMV of a massive coronary.""What the hell are you talking about? Is this some kind of joke? Did Billy set it up?"

"Here is your number, sir." She handed over a ticket. J1329.

"Look here, I asked for the same number. I have been waiting long enough. You are going to close before this number comes up.""Sir, you have only just arrived. And we never close." She waved her hand and yelled, "NEXT," and I looked behind me to see a big line had formed since I'd been standing there. I was rudely pushed out of the way by a fat lady on a walker and I stood there looking up at the monitors.

Now serving Number A192, a voice rang out from the speakers over the hum of the huge room. "Now serving Number A192 at Window 18." I looked around. The room was bigger than I remembered. Way bigger. This was the worst day ever. Number J1329?! I may as well go home. There was no way I was fixing the damn registration.

I may as well go home, drive Harry the dog to the dog park and check out the chicks who bring their prized mutts to the dog park. Harry can run around trying to get some game with some cute little Australian shepherd. Then we'll drive home.

I'll make some steaks and Harry and I can get in our lazyboys and enjoy a couple of good steaks and watch some YouTube documentaries. Sounds way better than wasting another hour or two here and them closing the place on me long before I get to my number.

I walked back towards the door. But I must have gotten turned around 'cause I couldn't see it. There was a young couple sitting on the ground where the door should have been and they were crying. The DMV seemed a little more dramatic than normal. I walked up to a guard in uniform. He was tall, probably closer to seven feet than six, and in his youth he may have played basketball, but he was in his late 60s now. It's not often I meet someone taller than myself, so I felt a certain amount of instant respect for the size of the man.

"Hey, look, I wanna go home.""We all want to go home."

"Yes, well, I am sure you can at the end of your shift. I just want to go home now and I can't seem to locate the door."

"There is no door."

"There is no door? What do you mean? What kind of DMV is this? You're the security guard. Help me."

"I'm not the security guard, just in work clothes." He pointed to the name on his shirt, Brinks.

"Oh, so you're just waiting here too. How do I get out of here?""You can never leave."

"This prank has definitely gone too far. Billy, where are you? Hotel California lyrics? You aren't even original."

"Sir, this ain't a prank." He pulled out a chair. "Here, sit down." I did as ordered because one does not say no to the biggest man in the room. "Son, you aren't leaving. I'm not leaving. This isn't a DMV. You is dead. I'm dead, you're dead, we are all dead."The humor seemed to have been sucked out of the room."But if this isn't the DMV..."

"Take a look around you. You ever seen a DMV this big?"I looked about and realized that the room was not just big, or even huge, it was endless. I hadn't really processed it till now. I was in an endless room filled with plastic fucking chairs and people waiting with tickets in their hands."Where the fuck am I?"

"Best as I can figure this is purgatory."

"Purgatory? Like Hell?"

The old man shook his head. "You ain't never been churched, have you, boy?"

"Nope." I shook my head. I mean, there was that spell when my grandmother was dying that we went to church a couple of times with her, mostly I think so my dad wouldn't get cut out of the will, but I couldn't really remember too much except being bored and my shoes being too tight.

"Well, I figure I got the time to school you now. I'm Alf. What's your name?""Charlie. How long you been here, Alf?""Not sure. More than a day, less than a month, I think. Time doesn't seem to work the same. There are no clocks. I don't feel hungry, or tired. Nothing hurts. For years I've been walking around on my job with a burning ache in my right foot, and a kind of stiffness in my knee and shoulders. And well, it's gone. I still feel like it's me but without any pain."

Now that he mentioned it, my body did feel different; lighter, without aches anywhere. The tightness in my back was gone and I wasn't tired anymore. I didn't remember the last time I hadn't felt tired.

"Yeah, it's weird. If we're dead, why are we still in the same clothes? I am sure you don't want to be in uniform."Alf smiled. "I been thinking about that. Seems to me that everyone is still wearing the same thing they wore when they died, so same clothes, same bodies, same hearing aids, same walkers. If you look around, most of the people here are on the older side.

You are actually here a little young.""She said heart attack, at the DMV. Can you imagine? Must have caused quite a kerfuffle."

"Yep, that's a piss-poor place to die. There's little clubs here and there, based on where or how you died. The COVID club is in front of Window 90. They discuss vaccine inefficiencies of all things. Then there's the Death by Nursing Home Accident club; they are a pretty big club. And of course, the Fuck, This Suicide Attempt Worked club. They are one sorry bunch of fuckers. Don't think there's a DMV club.""Suicide is bad, right? I mean, for getting to Heaven, or—""Hell. Yep. Well, I don't know if there is a Hell, or Heaven, or what this place really is, but I was raised to believe that after we died we went to purgatory. Like, this halfway place between life and the afterlife. If you wasn't good enough to get straight to Heaven, then you went to purgatory and were cleansed by holy fire so you could then go to Heaven.""Holy fire? Like Hell?""Not really, but what difference does it make? I look around and don't see any fire.""Nope. Looks like a DMV.""Exactly. I think that maybe we are serving our punishment needed to get to Heaven just by sitting waiting for our number."

"So I was right; this is Hell."Alf threw his head back and let his whole body laugh. A few people turned around to stare, to see if he'd actually gone insane and was about to hurt them, I suspected. When they realized he was really laughing, a few people joined in. It was that kind of bone-shaking, start-at-your-feet laugh, and I even found myself giving a chuckle.

"Oh, thank you, Charlie. I needed that. But actually, so far as I can figure it, Hell is through one of those doors over there..."He pointed. There were four doors set behind the windows, kind of like portals more than doors, or maybe like those metal detectors in the airport, the new ones where everyone stands looking silly with their hands up and their legs spread. Same kind of position you'd be in to be in a porn film, or a lynching, a pose about as natural as the limbo.

"So, two doors to Hell? And two doors to Heaven?"Eddie shook his head. "I don't think so. I think it's one door to Heaven, one to Hell, one to rebirth and the last one who knows?""Rebirth?

"Yep. From what I can tell, if you haven't been bad enough or good enough you just go back and try again."

I groaned. "Don't tell me the bloody new-age hippies were right and we have to go do this thing all over again."

"Well, I could be wrong," said Alf.

But somehow I knew he wasn't. He'd been walking around watching things long enough in life he knew how to look for patterns, and if he'd watched this mess and worked out some people were reincarnated, well, then maybe they were. And here I was somehow getting used to the idea I was dead, and that I could go to Heaven or Hell, and he was throwing a whole new spanner in my fruit salad.

Over the next few days Alf and I got really close. He should have been a preacher or a leader of men. I mean, like a good leader of men; not just some smarmy politician but someone with a soul, who actually cared. It may have been days, I think, or weeks; time was flexible.

We wandered up in boredom to watch the proceedings, getting some seats in front of Window 193. "Now serving I324 at Window 193."

A young man, still stoned, with vomit on his shirt, walked up. We couldn't hear him but he was handed a piece of paper. He looked down at it, confused, and was directed behind the window to a man who took the paper and pointed to which door he needed to go to.

"Suicide door to Hell," I said.

"Not so sure stupidity counts as suicide," said Alf.

"Oh come on, if you take the shit yourself you got to know you could die.""The one time I OD'd I had no idea it was possible," said Alf.

"You what," I said, turning to my friend, confused. "Yeah. When I was young I sold crack cocaine. Took too much one day, ended up in hospital, then prison.""Prison?" I looked him up and down. He looked like a good person. How could he have been in prison? My whole view of the world shifted. I was dead. My best friend was a jailbird waiting for entry to Heaven, and I knew nothing.

"Yep. Spent six years. Lost my wife, my kid, had to start again when I got out."

"Oh." I couldn't think of anything else to say. The young man headed towards door three.

We watched the doors and guessed that door one was Heaven, door two was Hell, and door three was reincarnation. It was the most used door. Door four wasn't used too often and we really weren't sure what it was used for at all. Actually, the door to Hell wasn't used a whole bunch either, but when you see a string of tattooed skinheads with swastikas going in the same entrance you got to figure it's not necessarily anywhere you really want to go. Especially when a rather famous televangelist most famous for child molestation and suicide before jail also followed them. We were pretty sure at that point it was definitely Hell.

The Heaven door wasn't used for the people I thought it would be. The ones who sat on their knees praying to God/Vishnu/Buddha/Mohammed all over the room rarely passed through that portal. We got to the point where we would bet, and I was the best at picking where people would go.

A nun walked up to the desk. She was bent over and serious. She walked up crossing herself as she went.

"I bet reincarnation," I said.

"Heaven," bet Alf.

Alf always thought people were better than they were. "You thought the last one was Heaven too."

"True, that."I was right—the reincarnation. The next woman was a short cleaning lady still wearing her hotel staff uniform and carrying the bucket, with a smile on her face. "Heaven," I said.

"Really?" said Alf. "I suppose you think that you and I are going to Heaven too?""I am definitely not," I said with certainty. "But I would put money on you going.""Not with my past."The cleaning lady walked into Heaven with her cleaning pail still in hand.

"I don't think it's about your past," I said. "I think it's something different. I think you have it, and I know I don't."

Alf turned to me and said, "It will be ok, Charlie. You'll be fine."

I looked over at Alf sitting there peacefully, watching the world. He'd been to prison, lost his family, sold drugs, almost OD'd, but I was sure looking at him that he was going to Heaven. He'd spent so much of his life watching, waiting for bad people to do bad things, but he wasn't bitter.

"Look at that old lady over there, Charlie. She's been here longer than me. She's walking around looking for someone. We don't have anything else better to do; why don't we help her look?""Sure," I said, not because I really wanted to help anyone, but I didn't have anything better to do. And Alf had helped me. So I followed him over to the old lady.

She was bent over a walker. Her oversized shirt was embroidered in little animals and the shirt underneath was still stained with whatever the last meal she'd eaten had dripped on her shelf of a bosom. Her little legs were shriveled up underneath her and moving about was a shuffle, even with the walker.

"Have you seen this man?" she said, pointing to a locket around her neck, which I now saw was open to show a picture of an old man. "It's my Frank. Have you seen my Frank?"

"Sit down, honey," said Alf. "We'd like to help you look.""Oh, that would be very nice." She turned her walker and sat down on the seat built into it. "I could use some help.""Well, we'd like to help you. How long have you been looking?" Alf sat down on a nearby chair and looked straight at her face.

"I'm not sure. My Frank died just a few days before I did. In bed, you know, just woke up and he was dead. I mean, they say isn't it nice that he died at home in his sleep, and he never suffered, but they don't talk about what it's like to wake up next to a corpse."

"No, they don't.""And I told him to wait for me. I mean, I wasn't picturing this exactly. I sort of thought he'd be in Heaven but here we are, and I told him to wait, and I'm sure he has. I mean, it's not like the line runs quickly and well, he couldn't really run at all in the end. He should be here. Oh, but you don't know what my Frank looks like, do you? He's really a good-looking man, or he was, you know, before he got all hunched over and his hair fell out. I mean, he's ok-looking for 87, just not the man I married if you know what I mean. I mean, I thought we'd be in Heaven in our younger bodies. If I have to spend eternity pushing this damn walker around, I'm not sure I'm going to make it. Oh, and his walker is the same as mine. I sewed matching covers for both our walkers."

I looked at her walker carefully. It had a purple velvet seat cover; that must be what she was referring to. I mean, how hard could it be to find one elderly man in an endless room with old people as far as the eye could see, with a walker with a purple cover? I grimaced at Alf but he was not fazed.

Alf jumped up on a plastic chair, put his hands around his mouth and started to yell. "Hey, all you people, attention, please."

People turned to him with a loud clatter of moving plastic chairs and walkers. "What's your name, ma'am?" He looked down at the woman on the walker beneath him.

"Evelyn Gates. Well, I was born Evelyn Poeters but..."

Alf brought his hands back to his mouth, cutting her off by yelling again. "Please help. Mrs. Evelyn Gates is looking for her husband Frank Gates. He died just a few days before her. He's 87 years old and has a walker with a purple velvet cover. We are looking for Frank Gates."

Alf kept calling. It was interesting how quiet the room could become with one man commanding their attention. "Evelyn is looking for Frank Gates. We are standing directly in front of window 193. If anyone has seen or knows of Frank Gates' whereabouts, send him this way. Please, repeat the message so we can find him. Please help us find Frank Gates. Evelyn misses him."

Alf got down off his chair and a murmur went out into the crowd. I could see in the distance people standing on chairs to repeat the query. We sat down with Evelyn and the crowd got louder.

"Do you think we can find him? I mean, do you think people heard you? What if he's already passed over? I mean, I might have missed him—"

She would have kept going but Alf cut her off again. "We've done what we can, Evelyn. Now we just wait.""But, what if he—""No point in worrying, Evelyn. Tell me a bit about y ourself."Evelyn started into a long story about her grand-children—there were twelve—and her children—there were four—and her great-grandchildren—three with two on the way—and the home she and Frank had moved to when they couldn't cope with all the maintenance on their mobile home in the seniors' park in the desert. Evelyn started talking and just kept going. I was looking for Frank to save us from her, and I was seriously beginning to wonder if he was hiding. After 52.5 years married to this woman, I might have thought that death was a welcome relief. Or at least a vacation.

By the louder than normal people hum I was pretty sure that Frank would be found soon, unless he'd already passed over. I was kind of thinking a lifetime of Evelyn would have made him eligible for Heaven. I looked over at Alf and he was still listening intently to Evelyn's life story. "I was born right after the start of the great depression. My mother was a teacher and my father worked on the railroads. But they were both drinkers, so they would leave their jobs and we would move to the next town. I've lived in..." Oh my lord, she'd started at the beginning! This could take a while. I looked out into the crowd for some sign of our salvation, then back at Alf; he didn't seem bored. He seemed interested, and I realized when Alf's number got pulled, he just might be one of the few who went through the door to Heaven. He seemed to have it all worked out, and he was just such a better person than me.

A cheer rose up in the distance, like the wave at a sports event, and the message was passed on. We heard it as a whisper before we heard it as a cry, "Frank's here. Frank's on his way.""Did I hear that right?" asked Evelyn, putting a hand to her ear as if she were a little hard of hearing—but I suspected she wasn't, not anymore. I also suspected she didn't need the walker anymore, that it was just force of habit, like Alf wearing his security uniform and me slouching. For fun, I tried standing straight and found myself looking up over most of the crowd. Damn, I was so much taller that way. It had been years since I'd been able to stand up straight. It didn't even hurt, it felt easy—and then I slouched back down because it was habit, and because it felt like me.

"Yes, Frank is on his way here," said Alf, taking her hand and helping her to her feet.

I stood up straight again to see the progress. The crowd was parting to let Frank through. And he was walking with amazing speed for a man pushing a walker. The crowd was moving aside plastic chairs and pointing the way, and before Evelyn could hyperventilate completely and collapse, he had arrived. He dropped his walker and threw his arms around her."What are you doing here, baby?" he said into her ear.

"Didn't want to be without you," she said.

Alf grabbed my arm. "Well, we'll let you two be alone." He pulled me away and the couple started to kiss.

"That's not going to end well," I said.

"What do you mean?" asked Alf as we neared our original place near a sign that indicated they were now serving G123 at Window 281.

"Marriage—it always ends badly. Either they break up or they love each other forever, and one person dies and devastates the other.""But they are back together now.""Exactly. For how long? Who's to say she doesn't go to Hell and he goes to Heaven?"

"That won't happen," said Alf. "They are meant to be together.""Really? Why are you so sure?""I just am."

"Now serving A4502 at Window number 5," intoned the automated voice.

"What's your number, Alf?""A4502.""That's what I thought," I said. "Your number is up. Time to go to Window number 5."

"Oh, wow." He looked down at his number then up again at the board. The voice intoned the message again."Yeah." It was always that way, even at the DMV. When your number was finally up it hit you with surprise, like you'd forgotten why you were even waiting.

He started to walk. "You want to come with?""Sure," I said. "I ain't got anything better to do. And I was going to miss him. I didn't know how to wait without him now.

We walked through the aisleways down till I saw Window 5. He walked up and I stayed behind the red line. I wanted to walk up and stand next to him, but it was more because I was curious than anything.

He looked behind and smiled at me. The woman handed him a piece of paper and he walked back behind the booth towards the doors. Another person took the paper and directed him, and he walked up to and through the door we'd thought by looking belonged to Heaven. I sighed, not realizing till then that I'd been holding my breath. I'd been right. It was nice to know that Alf was one of the good guys. I was sure I wouldn't be following him, but it had been nice to know him.

I looked down at my hand. J1329. The ticket was pretty squished up by now. I looked up at the board. Now Servicing B1239 at Window number 93. Ever since they started pulling that shit where they have different letters as well as numbers it's been so damn hard to work out how long you'll have to wait.Although in this place it was hard to work out how long you already had waited. I hadn't been pee since I got there, or eaten, or I put my hand on my wrist, or apparently had a pulse. It was different.

"Now Serving J1328 at Window 53."

I might be next, or maybe I might be in a week or two. I walked back to where we had left the happily reunited couple.

"Frankie," called Evelyn, "this is Charlie, one of the nice young men who found you for me. Where's your friend Alf? Oh, actually, I don't know if you were friends, or just acquaintances or—""His number was called.""Oh my. Frankie's number is before mine but we've decided to walk up togeth er." "Even if we get sent different places, at least we'll have a few more moments together," said Frankie, who apparently, by the way, was looking at Evelyn like he really did love her.

"That's nice. I wish you both well."

"You shouldn't talk like that, Frankie; I am sure we'll be together no matter where we go."

"Yes, quite. Best of luck to you both," I said and walked off, not wanting to waste any more of their couple time. I sat there watching the booth windows and the doors. Door one, the one Alf had passed through, sure seemed like it probably went to Heaven. Door two definitely Hell, unless they were sending raving hatemongers to Heaven just to mess with things, door three where pretty much everyone went was the one Alf had guessed was for rebirth. And door four was just sitting there unused. Almost no one went that way. Maybe it was just the door to the janitor's closet.

I wondered how you got this job, day in day out. I mean, I wasn't sure why people would work at the DMV, but this was worse, an infinite stretch at the eternal bureaucracy. I looked at the information booth and it was the same woman permanently on post. There wasn't even a breakroom. I would need to ask when I got there. I mean, what were the perks of doing this job?

Maybe if you did time in the office, you got out of Hell. I mean, seriously, why else would you do this job?

"Now Serving J1329 at Window 86."

I could hardly believe it; it was my turn. I started walking towards Window 86. And as I walked up to the window, I saw the woman at the desk waving me in.

I handed over the ticket. "Thank you," she said. "Charles Wilson?" "Yes, Charlie Wilson."

"Ok, Mr. Wilson, here is your determination. Please walk to the next officer and give him the form, and you will be dire cted.""Which door am I going to?""That's not my job.""How did you get this job?""I applied, sir. Please move to the next position." She pushed a button, and an announcement rang out.

"Now servicing G10321 at Window G6."I looked at her, but she wasn't about to answer any more questions any more than the guy at the DMV was going to rip up your parking tickets. I knew I had to walk to the next guy in the line and hand him my form. And I was scared. I mean, I didn't think I was going to go to Hell, but I knew, as sure as ice cream melts in a fire, that I wasn't getting to Heaven. So, my guess was rebirth. But what if I was wrong, and what if I was sent to door four? I realized at this point that I was terrified, that I had been terrified since I realized I was dead. I wondered if I could just stay dead and in the in-between. Maybe that was what she'd meant by applying. Maybe I could just apply to work at the Dead DMV forever and never find out my fate.

I could hear Alf's voice in my head. "It will be ok, Charlie." So, I put one foot in front of the other till I reached the next stop and I handed over my paper, which looked blank to me, but the bureaucrat with a blank face of disgust at the world grabbed it and looked at it as if he could read it.

"Mr. Charles Wilson?""Yes."

"Door Four, please."

And now I could see numbers on the door—they just appeared—and he was directing me towards the door no one passed through, the last door in the options. Not Hell, probably, but not Heaven.

"Are you sure?""Yes," said the human automaton and pushed me not so gently towards the portal. I found myself being drawn into it, sucked in. This was why no one refused to go to Hell—because they had no choice. They were pulled in with or without consent. And I slid towards the door like I was on a moving sidewalk. I turned back to see the elderly couple at a window together and I wished them well. I closed my eyes and held my breath as I shot through the portal and out of limbo.

I hurt like hell. My chest felt like I'd been kicked by a mule and the smell of burning hair filled the air. This must be Hell, I thought. I looked down at my chest where my little chest hairs were smoking, and my nipples looked burned. I looked up, and an EMT was kneeling above me with two defibrillator paddles in his hands.

"Oww...""He's coming around," yelled the EMT. "Bring in a stretcher and we will take him to Olive View."I looked around. Bad fluorescent lighting, plastic chairs. I pulled my arm up, my number in my hand. It said number D134.

"Now serving Number D133 at Window Number 3."

The worst thing was that I was alive. I had been sent back to my own body, and I was going to have to come back to the DMV again to register the car. I would miss it when they called my number.

Hope

HOPE

//hOhp/ noun and verb

The idea that better things are possilbe and thus we
keep trying. Hope was the last and worst of the evils
let out of the box by Pandora. Hope is the soul
destroyer and the last thing people want to lose.

Chapter Five

The Checkup

My watch beeped. I was due for a medical. I hit the snooze button. Who has time for that kind of thing? I was already late for class. If I didn't get there soon the kids would be in the classroom before I was, drawing on the board with permanent markers like last time. The faint impression of a red penis was still on the right-hand side of the board despite scrubbing it down with alcohol and the official board-cleaning product. I ran into class disheveled, as normal, and threw my bag down on the desk. Two or three kids were already there but they weren't the troublemakers. If you have a class of 30, then 25 of them are good kids, 2 are fucking awful, and 3 are followers of the evil duo. I'd been teaching for 5 years now and it was always the same.

Last year I'd gotten my period during lunch and been three minutes late after the bell rang. Troublemaker number one was a typical future loser. He'd run back into the classroom with his minions, and the five of them had slid the active shooter lock. It's basically a metal slide bar that locks the door from the inside. Probably wouldn't actually stop a psychopath from shooting us all through the window. I wasn't a psychopath, yet all I could do was look through the window and see the five nine-year-old boys laugh and climb all over the chairs while the entire class and I knocked on the door. When they had finally had enough fun, they decided to let us in and couldn't muster the motor skills between them to let us into the room. They couldn't slide the bolt back.

At this point the whole school knew I'd been locked out of my classroom. My kids were making noise and the headmaster showed up while we were all still outside the classroom. I wasn't sure if he wanted to fire me, but I knew I wanted to quit. After some instruction and the janitor coming with a screwdriver, the door was finally opened. My lesson plan was shot, and I regretted all my decisions to teach yet again. But

I am still here, and there's another class of 4th graders trying to learn how to structure basic English and divide numbers bigger than 20.

Sometimes I am so damn glad we've never had kids. I mean, we were planning to but then we wanted a house and a career. And then it just didn't happen. It's not like we didn't try. Cameron said it was ok, that I was enough, and he said it like he meant it. I wonder sometimes what he would have been like as a kid in the classroom. I think he would have been the class clown, too smart to be paying attention, destined to never rise to his full potential but loved by his peers and also secretly by his teachers too.

We talked about adopting for a while. But it was just too hard; too few kids, too many parents who wanted them. So, we adopted two pit bull crosses. They are definitely easier to train than these kids.

My watch buzzed again. I tried the snooze, but it said, "Checkup could not be snoozed." I turned to the girl in the front row who always likes to kiss up. "Margaret, please read Page 23 to the class." Margaret started to read while I looked down at the damn watch. The full medical exam must be completed by the end of the week. Then it gave me three times I could reschedule. I picked the one after work; no point in dragging it out. I looked up at Margaret. She was only halfway down the page but it was so damn dull the troublemakers were getting ready to interrupt. "Thank you, Margaret. I will take it from here. So, class, what do you think the author meant when he talked about environment?"

My phone beeped confirmation of the medical appointment. I was glad medicine was socialized. My mom had told me that in her day, if you didn't have enough money, you never got to see a doctor in time to treat anything and you just died. This system was better but I wished it was less mandatory.

You didn't have to pay for any kind of treatment, but you had to do all the checkups required. Early detection could cure most diseases, so if you just refused to go get checked they refused to treat you and you died. That was what had happened with my mom. She was convinced that doctors had killed her mother and father, so she never went for the checkups. Even when her stomach started to turn hard and her body bloated outward, she still wouldn't go for a checkup. The state cancelled her medical insurance eight months before she died, but she would have died anyway. The cancer had already filled her intestinal cavity, consumed a kidney and smothered her liver. It was only her pure stubbornness that kept her alive as long as it did. I got some prescription marijuana. I told them I was depressed, and I gave it to her. It kept the pain down enough to let her die in her own bed. Checkups are good, I told myself as I started to write the homework on the board and heard the class moan.

"Write this down, children. If you don't have it ready to hand in first period tomorrow, then you will need to work through your lunchtime to complete it or stay after school on detention." It was never too early for the kids to find out that they had to do as they were told or there would be consequences. Life was impossible if you didn't learn to obey. Sometimes I still wish I was as disobedient as my mother. She'd never asked for obedience from me but I'd learned anyway, at school, from friends, from society. My mother had never fit into society, she'd never voted or paid taxes, or collected welfare. She'd gone from one man to another, leaving when it wasn't fun anymore. And in between we'd lived from whatever the garden provided or Granddad had been willing to give. I had sworn never to be like her. I always did everything I was supposed to do.

I ran to the checkup office, not wanting to be late, not even for a machine. The checkup office is so efficient you don't see a human at all unless there is something wrong. I lay down in the tube bearing my name. I scanned my chip and the cover closed.

I was starting to hyperventilate. I told myself not to panic. That this wouldn't take long, that the tube wasn't so small, and it had a glass plate to look out, that there was plenty of air. And the machines began to hum. A small prick and the blood was drawn, and the ultrasound and MRI began checking me for tumors. And I knew the real fear wasn't the tiny checkup tube—it was the results. What if they found a tumor—even a small one was sometimes inoperable—or something else? The machine was measuring my lungs and my breath, and I tried not to hyperventilate. I tried to breathe. I tried to think happy thoughts, but that was as elusive as always. So I thought about the upcoming test I was going to have to give the kids. The topic was photosynthesis and I had planned to make it a project. They would all have to grow a bean, then write about it. Then the headmaster said she wanted another test before the end of the quarter in science. I couldn't make them do a test and a project. The checkup was taking longer than normal. My panic started to grow.

If the machine found something small, it would fix it without you even knowing; use a laser to remove a pre-cancerous lesion, that kind of thing. So long as you didn't have to see a human you were ok. If after the checkup there was a doctor, then you were in trouble. Everyone knew that. The machine could do everything. The doctor was just there to give you the bad news, because no one had managed to make a machine that anyone wanted to hear they were dying from.

If the tube opened and there was a nurse or a doctor, it was bad. Really bad. The scanner scanned me again. Oh, shit shit

shit. The scanner went back, and the tube started to open. I closed my eyes and breathed in. I was just being paranoid. There was nothing to worry about. I was a perfectly healthy person, more or less. I mean I'd been nauseous in the morning lately, but that kind of thing happened. And there was that mole on my arm. I looked down. The mole was gone; they must have lasered it off. The lid opened completely and a woman in a long white coat was standing there. "Please come with me."

I threw myself out of the tube. Oh my god, oh my god, oh my god. It was a doctor. I mean, I knew they had offices in the back of the checkup station, but I'd never seen one. I'd never wanted to see one. I was numb already and I wanted to scream. She pointed to a chair, and I fell into it. I was dying. Maybe it was melanoma. Maybe that was what the mole was. Maybe I had cancer like my mother. But how could that grow so fast since my last checkup? Maybe it was my heart.

"We have your test results back. Mrs. Biakowski, is it?" I nodded. I'd been born Molly Green, but I was going to die Molly Biakowski. The only question was how long I had left. "I'm dying, aren't I?" I said.

"Well..." "Is it cancer? My mom died of cancer. What kind of cancer is it?" "It's not cancer, Mrs. Biakowski." "Then heart problems?"

"Please calm yourself. I will explain." "How can I be calm?" I wanted to jump over her desk and choke her.

"Mrs. Biakowski, you are not ill." The doctor smiled slightly.

"Then why am I talking to you?"

"At your last checkup we removed a fibroid from your uterine wall." "Yes?" I vaguely remembered that in the email showing the treatment I'd received. It had hurt for a while—another reason not to like the checkups.

"Well, Mrs. Biakowski," said the doctor, smiling. "You are right, usually I tell people they are dying, but you are fine. You are just pregnant.""Pregnant?""Yes, with twins." I realized in that moment how much I had been lying to myself. I had always wanted kids. I knew Cameron would be happy. But twins? How the hell was I going to cope with twins?

Chapter Six

Cassie's Curse

I saw her sitting on the cement stairs, lighting up. She'd taken to sneaking out of the house and smoking alone in the dark, sticky Florida nights. She took a long, quick drag, then threw the still burning cigarette into the yard and turned to me. "Stop smoking, Mom," I reiterated, touching her on the shoulder. "You know it'll kill you." You would have thought I could have made her listen. It was sensible advice.

"Leave me alone, Cassie. You know if I quit, I'll just get fat and then I'll die of a heart attack." At over 200 pounds, I could not really imagine my mother fatter, though she carried it well, the way big-boned women do; she looked strong and slightly masculine. "You don't want me to die of a heart attack, now, do you?"

"You'd prefer a long, lingering death of lung cancer, which turns into bone cancer? Every bone in your body aching, your hip snapping off as you creep around your house attached to your oxygen tank?"

"Oh Cassie, you worry too much," she said, lighting up another one just to prove she was right. "I'm not going to quit, and I'm not going to die of lung cancer."

But I knew she was. I didn't know how I knew things—I just did.

"Mom, I love you." "Yes, I know, but I am a grown woman. You look after you. I'll look after me."

Freddie lived next door to us. He was my best friend, at least until he turned five and discovered that girls were gross. I remember by fourth grade we were almost friends again. Our friendship was more complicated now. I wanted to touch his curly blond hair, and he wanted to show me how strong he was. We held hands when no one was watching, and he kept promising to kiss me. We were on our way home from school. It was a beautiful day, the kind you get right after summer vacation is over. Freddie let go of my hand and climbed up to walk on top of a high fence.

"Freddie, get off the fence, please," I called to him. It was a wooden fence that had once been white. "If you don't come down, you'll fall and break your neck." And even as I said it, I saw the picture in my mind. Little Fred Jackson was going to fall off the end of the fence. He would hit the ground at an odd angle and would spend the rest of his shortened life in a wheelchair.

"You sound like a teacher," he taunted me. "Well, Teach, what are you gonna do, keep me in for detention?"

"Please!" I screamed. "You don't understand! You have to get off the fence, now! Please!"

"Just make me," he yelled back.

"I don't want to see you hurt!"

"Miss Goody-Goody doesn't want me to get hurt!" He took one more step, then he fell. Just as I had seen, just as I had known he would. I could have stopped it, if only he had listened. But they never listen.

It was the first day of Junior High and Mom had insisted on driving me. "Mom, don't hug me."

"What? My little girl's too old to be hugged by her mom?"

"I don't want to be the only kid whose mom kisses her bye." That wasn't the real reason, but I'd given up on telling the truth to her. Every time she touched me, I saw her body, brittle and skeletal, decaying from inside. I'd told her a million times that the cigarettes would kill her, but she kept smoking. Now I just wanted to forget—I just wanted to get through the first day of a new school without starting the day with an image of death.

"Ok, baby, bye." She blew me a smoke-filled kiss. I heard a girl titter.

"Look, her momma walks her to school." Distracted by the malevolence of adolescence, I entered the school and pulled on my gloves.

It was five minutes into homeroom before the first girl asked me why I was wearing gloves. *So I don't have to see inside your life, so I don't have to know how you die.* But instead, I said, "I have a skin condition."

The idea of a hideous skin disease kept me successfully single throughout my painful puberty. Mom never knew I wore gloves everywhere but home. She was the only person I ever let touch me.

When I was sixteen, I saw a young woman looking at her reflection in the freezer section. I followed her to the makeup section. She stopped to look at herself again in a mirror, flipping her long, bleached locks over her shoulder.

In the mirror I saw the same reflection I had seen in the freezer door, the image of a scarred and scared woman, with broken teeth and blackened eyes. I hadn't even touched her, and I could see her pain. I walked up to her, shocked, too scared to think it through.

"Your husband will beat you," I told her.

"What?"

"Don't marry him. He'll hit you. You'll end up blind in one eye, your front teeth gone. He'll rip your hair out." The wounds from the final beating before she left him would never heal. That pretty, soft, young face would look like a road map when he was done with her.

"What!" She turned to me, her face pale. She nervously turned the engagement ring in her left hand. "You know Paul?"

"No. But he will cut your face up and leave you for dead."

"You're crazy." She ran, leaving her cart full of groceries behind.

Security found me in the next aisle, and I was held until the police came. She pressed charges. I was young so the judge dismissed them, but they put me in lockdown for one night—for a psychiatric evaluation.

The rooms were filled with pained souls. I could feel their suffering; I could see their deaths. The cell next to me contained an old woman; she couldn't remember a life outside of the institution. She would die a lonely death of old age, one of the forgotten left inside to rot. The other cell held a young man; after taking his prescription he would slam his head repeatedly into the wall until he died of internal bleeding.

The shrink tried to pretend he was my friend. I sat in his dark office, staring at the dirty gray carpet. I didn't tell him his wife was going to leave him. I didn't say anything. I was scared by everything I knew, and I was learning not to talk.

Mom came. She told them that watching my elementary school boyfriend fall from a wall had traumatized me. "The school counselor said she feels guilty and responsible because she didn't stop him," she whispered to the shrink.

I said nothing and stared past him at the wall. I was going to have to be more careful in the future. This power within me was growing. Now I could sense visions from people not only touching me but just in a close proximity. I didn't want to end up in a sanitized, rationalized jail for the rest of my days.

No one in the family spoke of Aunt Lynette. She'd died in a similar "hospital" just before I was born. She hadn't understood the virtue of silence and had been murdered by doctors performing a routine lobotomy.

"I'm very sorry if I said anything to upset anyone," I said with my mouth closed as I looked down at my feet.

"There, you see, she's sorry. Now can I take her home? She has exams coming up and this is a very stressful time. I am sure she was just reacting to all the stress..." The doctor also knew the virtue of silence and didn't respond. "You know I just want to take her home. If you want to give her some pills or something, if you think that will help, I'll make sure she takes them." At first, I tried taking the pills. The visions stopped; everything stopped. I felt like I was thinking through a sea of mud. I sold the pills to a young man who would die of a heart attack in his forties. But at least my pills wouldn't kill him.

Now the occasional flash of premonition was a thing of the past; everywhere I looked I could see the future. When I opened my eyes, I saw not only the present, but also any pain in the future of whoever I looked at. The only future I could not see was my own.

I wanted to help people. It made sense that I had been given this gift for a reason. I must be able to change the future, otherwise I wouldn't be able to see it. But no one would listen. Nobody wanted to know how bad it could be, how much pain the future could hold. Perhaps there was no one strong enough to change his or her fate, or perhaps fate is immutable. I don't know. I only knew that I didn't want to end up like Aunt Lynette.

I tried not to see, tried to block out the sea of images everyone carried, but occasionally one would land in front of me full borne. Visions of death. I prayed for this "talent" to just go away. I couldn't just go up to strangers and scare them; I needed a way to try to change the future anonymously.

The first note, I slid into Susie Simon's locker before school. It read, "Don't sleep with Grant Fletcher."

I stood back, watching as she opened her locker. She took the note out and read it. "Hey, Tammy," she yelled to her friend. "Look at this!"

Tammy came over. "Ugh, Grant; as if you ever would. I mean..."

"Exactly. He's totally not my type. Like..."

I walked away, convinced that the note had worked. I ran to Grant's locker to see if he had gotten his note, but class was already starting and the hall was clear. Grant and Susie wouldn't have sex, the retarded baby wouldn't be born, and Grant wouldn't kill himself. I had stopped the whole chain of events.

The next warning, I wrote on the wall of the girls' changing room. LISA, DON'T TAKE ECSTASY! IT WILL KILL YOU. I knew she would read it and she would be saved.

I felt happy and carefree. There must be a reason for my talent. I must have been put on earth to change things, and for a couple of months I believed I had.

"Did you hear?" whispered Amy in English class. Mr. Call was late again, and she could have spoken at full volume but Amy's voice always dropped to a whisper for particularly meaty morsel of gossip.

"Did I hear what?" I replied.

"Susie Simons is pregnant, and they say Grant Fletcher is the father."

"NO!"

"Oh, yes. There's no way she would have slept with him sober, but apparently he slipped her a ruffie."

"Fuck!"

"Cassandra!" yelled Mr. Call, walking into the class. "Excuse me. Is there something you would like to share with the class?"

The class laughed. "Sorry, sir." I put my head in my hands.

Four weeks later Lisa Ganty died of an overdose of ecstasy.

I could see the future, but I couldn't make anyone listen. I just couldn't change it. I couldn't even stop my mom from smoking. I hid her cigarettes; I "forgot" to buy her a pack at the shop; I begged her, and I pleaded.

On my seventeenth birthday I came home from school early. I looked around the kitchen, the dining room, but there was no cake. I didn't expect a party; I didn't have any close friends, and there was no one I would have invited. But Mom always made me a birthday cake—a Duncan Hines box chocolate cake with chocolate icing and M&Ms. I walked into the bedroom, and she was lying there, motionless. Mom was never motionless; she was always moving, bustling about.

"Cassie."

She was going to tell me. I knew before the words left her lips. She was already getting thin, looking quite beautiful. The fat that had coarsened her features was gone and you could see her cheekbones, her shoulders.

"I went to the doctor today, and I have terminal cancer."

I went to the bed, lay down with her and put my arms around her. It was no time for "I told you so"; we didn't have enough time left for recrimination.

"I took out a life insurance policy three years ago. When I die, baby, you'll have a million dollars. I hope it's enough to keep you out of trouble."

"A million dollars?"

"If I'd asked for more they would have wanted a physical. I didn't know if I would pass the physical."

"But, life insurance?" She felt small in my arms, more like my child than my mother. It wouldn't take long now before she was gone. I wanted to hold her and stop her from slipping away from me.

"Cassie, baby, I knew you were right. On some level I always knew. But you can't change fate. This is my fate."

"Oh, Mommy." I just cried, and she held me and comforted me, pulling me to her shrunken bosom.

"At least when I'm gone, you'll be ok," she said. I was sure I would never be ok again.

I met Todd that month. I saw him coming out of the surf. He was eighteen and destined to die at age twenty in a car accident. I went to the beach at dawn every day, just to watch the waves, write in my journal and see the sunrise. His golden sinuous beauty was just a bonus. As he walked out of the waves his skin glistened.

"Hey, you surf?" he asked me.

"No."

"Why are you here every day?"

"Just to watch the water. It's beautiful."

He sat down beside me and said nothing. He seemed to understand that I needed the calming sound of the waves more than I needed him to speak.

The next day he joined me on the beach again and soon we were lovers. I brought him home to the house. Mom was happy I wasn't alone; she didn't have to sit in the living room with me and pretend she was ok. She would greet Todd with a cigarette-smoke kiss and retire to her bedroom to die a little more.

When he was touching me, I could forget. Forget for a moment, a pure moment of sensation without thought. His hands would run up and down my body. I'd never been touched, never been kissed. And in the aftermath of pleasure the visions would return.

"What's wrong?" he said, leaning over to me, his eyes half closed, his lips swollen with kisses, his body sticky with sweat.

"What if I told you I could see the future?"

"I'd ask you what the lotto numbers were." He smiled a slow, languid smile and started to nuzzle my breast.

"No, I'm serious," I said and sat up, pushing him away. "I see visions of death. I see how people are going to die."

He looked at me for a moment, then swallowed.

"How am I going to die?"

"In a car crash."

"When?"

"In about two years."

He nodded. Then he reached into his bag. He pulled out a joint, lit it and gave it to me. "This should take the edge off." I puffed. "No, inhale deep, then pass it over; it's not every day I get told how mortal I am."

"I'm sorry," I said and passed the joint to him. My head felt light, my brain fuzzy.

He smiled down at me. "You have beautiful breasts."
****

"I'm glad to see you so happy, baby," said Mom. She was in the hospice now; she needed care to get through the days and the endless nights. I didn't tell her the truth. I didn't tell her that the only way I was getting through the days myself was by never sobering up. My head was a fuzzy mess of vodka and pot, but at least I could bring myself to visit her, tiny and pale in the big, white death cot. "Todd must be doing you some good."

"Yes, I suppose he is." We spent every minute available together. He was with me everywhere but this antiseptic coffin of the living dead.

"Does he know about, well, about..."

"Yes, he knows everything about me and about the visions. He loves me anyway."

She nodded.

The phone rang that night. I reached across Todd, already knowing what they would say. "Ok, I'll be right there."

I started to dress. Todd sat up and reached out to me. "What's wrong?"

"She's gone into a coma. They are going to turn the oxygen off. I need to go hold her hand when she dies."

"I'll come with you," he said, getting out of bed.

"You don't have to."

He put his arm around my shaking body. "Yeah, I do."

Her room felt like it was already empty. She lay tossing on the bed.

"I thought someone in a coma would look peaceful, like they were asleep," Todd said.

"Me too." But she looked like she was in pain, fighting for breath, thrashing about like a fish on a dock. They turned off the oxygen and turned up the anesthetic. The thrashing stopped and she submerged from view.

The summer after her funeral, Todd and I went north, out of the cities, away from the people. I thought it would be easier. "You know," he said as he drove. "Not all prophecies come true."

I sat up straighter. "What do you mean?"

"Everything doesn't have to happen." He picked up a book from between the seats. "Even the most famous prophets aren't always right. One theory is that prophets are the voice of God. It's a gift from God, given to the pure of heart so that they can tell people what is coming—so that they can change things."

"There is no God."

"Cassie, are you sure?"

"If there were a God, things would make sense. If there were a God, my mom would still be alive. This is no gift, and I am not pure of heart. Pass me the vodka." He passed it back and I drank as much as I could swallow, but I wanted to believe. I wanted to believe that there was some reason, that I could change things. I needed hope, because nothing else could keep me from killing myself.

Todd pulled the car to the side of the road. He turned the engine off and took me in his arms. "Cassie, maybe they are wrong. Maybe this isn't a gift from God, but there must be a reason."

"Why didn't you just run when I told you you were going to die?"

"Why? I've always known I'm going to die. Now I'm just trying to live." He started to kiss me, and we made love in the car that night, sleeping on the side of the road. He woke me early the next morning. "What if you are God?"

"What do you mean?"

"There have always been prophets. The Bible is based on them, the Romans and Greeks talked about them. Maybe there are hundreds of prophets, and maybe they aren't the voice of God. Maybe, just maybe, nothing happens until it is prophesized."

"You mean I made Freddie and my mom die?"

"No. They had a choice. They had free will. You prophesized the possibilities and they chose to fulfill your prophecies."

"Self-fulfilling prophecies?"

"Maybe."

"Maybe I'm just insane and there have been coincidences."

"That would be easier than the truth, wouldn't it?" He kissed me. "It's going to be all right."

I discovered that there is nowhere to run. We rode up through Vermont, but always there were little towns, little villages. And people. People whose destinies lay before me, raw and messy. We came back before the first snowfall.

We moved to New York City where I found the sheer number of people made the visions blur into each other. I tried not to be alone with anyone except Todd. My mother's money bought us an easy life. He was accepted at NYU but couldn't apply himself. It's hard to study for a future you know you don't have.

"Cassie," he said, "I'm not going to die."

"But—"

"I know—your mom, Freddie, that girl we met in Essex Junction who fell off the horse, my friend Stu... But they didn't listen to your warnings. I have."

I reached out to him, feeling his despair in his denials. "Why don't I buy a boat? We'll sail out of New York on your birthday and keep sailing until you're 21."

"Maybe." He turned and picked up another book. "You know I was just reading, and I wonder if this gift of yours is a test."

"A test?"

"Yeah, maybe it's just God's way of testing to see—"

"Todd, I don't think there is a God."

"Well yeah, there's that." He kissed me, wet and desperate. "Maybe we should buy a yacht."

By the next day he'd changed his mind about the boat. It was his 20th birthday in four days and suddenly he seemed calmer, more at peace. I bought the ingredients to bake a cake—Duncan Hines, with chocolate icing and M&M's. I called as I walked in the door, but he didn't answer. I didn't know he was in the bedroom until I went in to go to the bathroom.

He lay slumped on the bed, note in hand, empty bottle of pills and spilled vodka on the bed.

I grabbed for the note.

Cassie, I will always love you. Make your own fate. I have. Love, Todd.

I started to scream. Then I knew. His fate hadn't changed; he was still going to die in a car accident. Putting my ear to his mouth I could hear his breathing, slow, shallow. I called 911.

By the time they arrived I had screamed hoarse. Todd's clothes were wet with my tears. He would be ok, they said, at least this time. I rode with him to the hospital. They pumped his stomach while they made me wait outside.

The emergency room was filled with pain. I watched three medics work on an overweight businessman whom they would not be able to save. I wanted to scream "STOP, don't waste your time; it's not worth the effort." But they ran around, defibrillators in hand, doing what they could do, what they were trained to do, while his wife stood shocked into stillness, watching her husband die.

"Cassandra." I turned. A young black nurse in blue walked towards me. "Hi. Todd is doing alright. He's going to be ok, but it will be a few hours before he comes to. Go home, get some sleep."

"Ok. What time can I pick him up?"

"Well, he's going to have to stay for a few days for observation."

"Observation."

"Yes, and psychiatric evaluation. He did try to kill himself."

They were going to tie him down and send him to a padded cell. The sanest person I'd ever met was going to be locked up because of me. I had to leave him. I had made him do it; I killed all the people I loved. By the time Todd came to in the hospital I had already packed and moved out of the apartment.

I found a basement apartment in Chinatown, the air and walls so thick with humanity that their fates were the buzz of bees in a swarming hive.

And so, the years passed. Two years ago, I was in Times Square, my favorite place, and I was hit by a wave of visions coming from all around. Visions of malnutrition, of deaths impossible in such an affluent society. I looked around me and tried to see the futures of the people wandering up and down Times Square, and suddenly all of their futures were fused. Their dissimilar lives would end similarly. The young black man pushing the stroller would starve to death. His baby would be a preschooler when it happened, and she would die of malnutrition and pneumonia only days later.

The old woman in front of me, the wide one with the limp, would freeze to death in her four-story walk-up. What was going on? This just didn't make sense. Visions of ice, cold, hunger and pain made me fall to my knees in front of Toys R Us. Was I finally going insane, imagining things that could not be?

I looked up to see the news. That was when I saw him. Mr. Leonard White. The caption read, "Former Governor Leonard White announces his candidacy in the Presidential Elections." I knew then that with that decision to run for office, Mr. White had changed the fate of the world.

Mr. White may look good on TV but he would never understand America's place in the world. A well-meaning public who thought he would tax them less would elect him. He would be the president who restarts the war with North Korea and helps Pakistan take Kashmir from India. His environmental policies would add to the atmospheric pollution. With that and nuclear war between India and Pakistan, the dust and radiation would seep into the atmosphere. The dust in the high strata would cause an ice age. Eighty percent of the world's crops would perish, along with ninety percent of its peoples.

Global images started to form. I could see the floods in Bangladesh, the children starving in Texas, the snow burying the northern states until they became glacier plains. The land bridge to Russia would reappear, but there would be no one to walk it. The ships that move food around the world would sink in massive, ice-driven storms. Apples from New Zealand, grapes from Chile would be lost, frozen in ice drifts or just sunk on the wild seas. The Gulf Stream would stop and England and much of Europe would freeze.

I must be insane. It wasn't possible; it couldn't happen. More visions poured into my head, and I knew. I knew, just as I had known about Mom.

This man couldn't be elected. I had to stop him.

I had never felt more alone.

I started to scream. No words, just the pain of the world to come. I sat in front of the Toys R Us with tears running down my cheeks. I watched young kids ride the Ferris wheel and I tried to concentrate on the spinning colors instead of the fates of the riders. My sobbing slowed and I got into a cab. The images of devastation flickered through my brain to the beat of the middle-eastern chanting on the stereo.

At home I went to my bathroom cupboard and opened a bottle of tranquillizers. I considered seeing how many I could swallow with vodka, but just took enough to sleep. Not everything prophesized comes true, I told myself. Todd always said people had free will. That fate was changeable.

Dan Brown was running against White in the Primary. I didn't believe in him. I didn't think he was a good man, just another politician. The lesser of evils, and with our political system he would be the first line of attack White would have to overcome. I went to his campaign office the next morning.

Lisa, who was standing at the front desk, greeted me. She was dressed in the same pale blue linen suit she had been wearing since the eighties. She was too thin, wound too tight for the comfort of herself or others.

"Hello. I'm Lisa Spangler. Can I help you?" The smile was permanently affixed, painted on each day over the decay.

"Hi. I want to work on the campaign."

"We can always use volunteers." She handed me over a clipboard. "Here, fill this out. I'll be right back." And she sprang out and grabbed a ringing phone. The headquarters were located in an old warehouse, temporary and ill-conceived.

Phone lines dangled from the ceiling and phones sat untended on long, barely manned tables.

Lisa popped back in and took my clipboard from me. "Oh, you have no experience, no degree, no work history..."

"No."

"Well, we'll keep you busy anyway."

And they did. I stuffed thousands of envelopes until I learned that my hands were independent of my mind. I would sit and think. I would wonder where Todd was, if he were still alive. The envelopes would pile up, done by robotic commands I was unaware of, much as I was unaware of breathing. Sometimes I would wake up at the table, my finger bleeding, only to find I had been working the whole time—only my mind had been visiting the end of the world.

"Why did you volunteer?" asked the aging hippie pervert next to me. I already knew why he had—because he didn't need to work, and he wanted to get out of the house and hit on women.

I thought for a moment, and then I realized, why not tell the truth? They weren't going to send me to a lockdown facility. They needed me to stuff their envelopes, make phone calls to people who didn't speak English, and donate enough money to keep this office open.

"I volunteered because I know that Mr. White is going to start World War III and the resulting nuclear winter is going to kill off most of the peoples of Earth."

"Well, yeah, he's probably stupid enough for that; and then there's his abortion stance. I mean, he's going to try to overturn *Wade v. Roe*, and you know that this president is going to be able to appoint at least three Justices to the Supreme Court because they are all getting so damn old, and the ones he appoints will all be pro-life. I mean, he's going to take a woman's right to choose, and as a woman you've got to be worried about that one. It'll be backyard abortions and women dying of septicemia all over again if this guy gets elected."

Why is it people only hear what they want to hear? What difference did abortion rights make? I smiled patronizingly at him. He continued talking, the sound of his own voice filling his own personal void. He'll die quickly, freezing to death when his van skids off the road and slides into the Hudson. I didn't tell anyone else in the office—there didn't seem to be any point.

We'd been at the office 19 hours straight by the time the results started coming in. The polls had said it was close, that anyone might win. But I didn't need pollsters. I didn't need CNN to give me the exit poll numbers. When I looked around at the anxious faces of the people I had worked with for weeks I could see the end, their end, an end Mr. White would bring.

I left the building before the wave of hugs and consolation was over. There was nothing I could do as a political volunteer to change the outcome, so I gave up on traditional methods. On the way home I purchased a can of red paint. I wrote across a wall in the 50th Street station, "Don't vote for White. He will kill us all." The paint ran. I threw away the can and jumped on a train before the police could arrive.

I walked back and forth on the train, unable to sit. I waved my red hands—my new stigmata—at people in their seats. "DON'T VOTE FOR WHITE," I screamed at the men reading their papers. "PRESIDENT WHITE WILL START WORLD WAR THREE," I yelled at the wannabe black boys with the oversized jeans. "IF WHITE WINS THE ELECTION WE ALL DIE," I screamed at the thin, tailored, young Jewish women and the rounded Yentas.

They stared through me as if I were furniture. The paint on my hands caused more interest than the words from my mouth. I could feel the policeman coming. I knew that a cop (destined to retire in only three months, from a gunshot wound) was walking towards me. They would put me away. Ask me questions and lock me up forever as an annoyance, conveniently swept aside. Doctors would want to know why I thought the way I did; I'd be silent. I pushed out through the train doors as it left the 42nd Street station and ran up to the street and into a waiting cab.

My exhaustion had taken me too close, too far. I knew I hadn't changed a single opinion, just scared some people on their way home. I looked down at my hands covered with my shame; by now the wall would be clean again. What had I been thinking? Did I really want to end up committed, bouncing off rubber walls or strapped to a gurney? It would be easier to quit now, just quit. Find some pills, some dope—something—and just float in a haze, waiting for the inevitable.

I poured nail polish remover on my hands and cleaned them as well as I could. Then I ran a bath. I soaked in the hot water pouring tequila down my throat. I wanted to cry, but the tears wouldn't come. I don't remember going to bed, but I woke late the next day with the taste of bile and a stabbing headache.

I turned on the television to be sure. "America needs a strong leader," said White, smiling. "The election results show that many Americans feel that I could be that leader. To take this country on a new path..." I turned it off, surprised that I had watched him for so long. The man was well intentioned, charismatic and eloquent. A pity he was also arrogant, self-righteous, and destined to destroy mankind.

I put an ad in the paper and hired a computer whiz. He made a website: Free Porn and Political Enlightenment. For five thousand dollars more he created a computer virus that told people not to vote for White. I couldn't make even the computer programmer believe, but he took the money.

I decided to audition for American Idol so I could have a venue for my message. Television was the only medium people believed, the only holy seer of the modern age, and I knew I must get on it any way I could. I wore a T-shirt to the audition that read, "DON'T VOTE FOR WHITE. HE WILL LEAD TO THE DOWNFALL OF THE HUMAN RACE." I can't sing, so I planned the only sensible thing—to sound as bad as possible so that I would make the "terrible/worst ever" cut and get my 15 seconds of fame.

It must have been a slow week because Channel Nine had a news team covering the people waiting for the auditions. I had lined up two days early so I would be at the front of the line.

"Well, hello," said the young news reporter, noticing only my breasts, not the words emblazoned upon them. "Would you like to tell us a little about why you're trying out for American Idol? Would you like to sing for us?"

"I can't sing."

"Then, why are you here?"

I looked straight in the camera.

"I can see the future. There are 5 deaths I can document having predicted, and I need to tell people not to vote for Mr. White as President, because he will start World War Three."

"Uh, huh. Well, best of luck." He ran a few steps down from me and soon a young Puerto Rican woman was belting out a tune. I walked up to the news reporter.

"When you get home tonight your wife will have left. And before she leaves, she will have poured salt in your fish tank. All your fish will be dead."

"Are you crazy?"

"No, and if what I told you is true, please contact me." I took a card out of my pocket and gave it to him.

The audition was traumatic, even though I knew it wouldn't be fun and that I wasn't any good. Somehow, standing in front of the judges, suddenly it felt important. For a moment I forgot my visions and centered only on my fear and the sweat covering me. I was dismissed quickly, probably not bad enough to make the cut for the show. I went home and showered until there was no hot water. I heard the phone ringing as I stepped out.

"Hello"

"Hello. Cassie?"

"Yeah?"

"You were right about the fish. Can you really prove that you know things?"

"Yes."

"Are you available at 11 a.m. for an interview?"

"Yes."

"Great. I'll meet you in the lobby and take you through security. Do you know where we are located?"

That was it; I was going to get to talk on television. How would I say it, how could I make them understand? All they had to do was change their votes to alter their future. It was only a local channel, but it could be picked up by a network. I would finally be able to tell people, to change things.

The young newsman led me to the bitter old harridan who was the star interviewer of the channel. She'd been demoted from the majors and resentment filled her twisted smile.

"Hello," she said, not rising from her chair.

I leaned into her and whispered in her ear, "You haven't told anyone about the breast cancer yet, have you?"

After that the interview was painless. Instead of attacking, she asked the questions that I knew how to answer. It was only a three-minute piece, but they ran it on the morning, afternoon and evening news. I watched it every time it came on. Did I look insane? Should I have worn a black dress instead of the jeans and slogan-covered T-shirt? Then again, if I hadn't worn the T-shirt would they have completely ignored what my message was and just centered on the fact that I was a prophet?

It was 9 a.m. when Harry, the TV producer, called. I suppose that isn't early for most people, but I spend every night drinking vodka and watching infomercials, too afraid of the visions that would come when I turn out the light; too afraid that the nightmares that form in the minutes before I go to sleep would follow into my dreams.

I couldn't understand who he was at first. "Cassandra, we want to base the show around you, your gift."

The show? What show? "I don't understand."

"We'd call it Cassandra – return of the prophet. The research we have done suggests that you don't preach or anything. No religious message, no voice from God?"

"No, I just see things."

"We think that would work. We'd have a studio audience; you could answer their questions. It would be a half-hour format, primarily for late night."

"A what?"

"A television show, national, with a post-news time slot."

"Ok." It sounded like a good idea. I figured it was a venue to get my message out.

By the following week Harry had dropped the Channel Nine interview into the pipeline. The network ran it on the primetime news while Harry's people fitted me out in wardrobe, and the ads for the new show began to air constantly.

The lead-in for the show showed pictures of Mom, pictures of some of the people I had known, pages from my journals showing proof that I knew things were going to happen. By the time the light show was over, even I believed I had a gift. The plan was that studio audience members would come and ask me questions.

The first one was ushered on stage. She was eighteen, with badly dyed hair and clothes that failed to hide the rolls of blubber. "I just want to know if I'm doing the right thing making Timmy marry me."

I looked at her twisting the engagement ring on her finger. I tried to say something useful but all I could come out with was, "It doesn't matter. Both you and Timmy will be weakened by starvation and freeze to death in your house."

"No, no, what you mean... I just want to know if we should-da get married..."

The stagehand walked her off stage.

Harry walked on. "Look, honey, I know you believe that, but Cassandra, this is television. You've got to give them some sugar with the medicine, you know."

I smiled at him. "I'll try." I reached over to the glass of vodka I had on the table in front of me and sucked it down.

"Can someone refill Ms. Cassandra's glass, please, and bring the next person up."

The next victim was an old woman, too old to do anything but vote against bills needed by the young.

"Dear, I just want to know if my Alfred is all right up there."

"I don't know."

"Well, ok. Do you know when I will be able to join him?"

"When the gas line breaks in the deep freeze, and you can't turn on the radiator in your room."

"I see." The old woman walked back to the stunned audience and sat down. Harry ran onto the stage.

"Look, honey, this just isn't working. On the off chance it didn't, I had a writer prepare a few answer suggestions. Jim!"

Jim the Writer ran on stage, papers in hand. He gave the papers to Harry and Harry gave them to me. He was going to leave but Harry's hand stayed him. I read through them quickly.

"Well, what do you think?" asked Harry.

"Do you want to know what I think about anything? Do you want to know what I see in your future?"

"Don't tell me," said Jim. "I really don't want to know." The truth was no one did.

"Harry, I quit. There is no way I am going to tell someone that their future holds romance and travel. If that is what they want to hear, they should just read their horoscope in the newspaper."

"But we have a contract," said Harry, the color rising in his face. "I'll sue you."

"Go for it," I said. "See if you can collect before the embolism in your head explodes." I walked out on the show, not realizing it had brought me a new kind of fame. Harry's advertisements and the news of the lawsuit had made me a toy of the television. I felt like no one could take me, the Ms. Clara of Manhattan, seriously.

Yet some believed and their letters reached me. As I read them I could feel the pain of the desperate people who wanted the world to end. More frightening than those was the one from a religious extremist who thought the end of the world would clear away the impure and leave only himself and his fellow hatemongers ruling the Earth. All he wanted from me was that I join his group and help him convert the masses to his cult.

I held the letter and looked at my apartment. Perhaps I should leave. Maybe I should move again. I had lived there three years, yet there were no pictures on the walls, no trinkets on the windowsill. I still slept in my sleeping bag on a mattress on the floor. My clothes lay in my open suitcases. The sofa was a hand-me-down and the 12-inch television worth nothing. I had never really arrived; it should be easy to leave. The phone rang and I picked it up. "Is this Cassandra?"

"Yes."

"Hi. My name is Elizabeth Mercer. I'm calling from *Newsweek*, and we'd like to interview you."

This was it, a serious news piece, not my name in the *National Enquirer* next to some Nostradamus quotes.

"Great. When would you like to meet me?"

"How about tomorrow at your home?"

"Ok, I'll give you my address."

How could I leave? This was my home. I was starting to make an impact. After this the election results would shift. I needed some place for people to contact me, and this was it. I looked around again. I had better clean up before they come, maybe shut the suitcases and hide them in the closet.

Elizabeth was well dressed, in a casual I-threw-it-all-together way. I looked down at my jeans and realized how long it had been since I had bought any clothes. "Hi. Come in." She walked in, escorted by a photographer. "Would you like a coffee, Coke, anything?"

"No, thanks." She looked me up and down. "You're not quite what I expected."

"Oh, sorry. I left my crystal ball and magic robes in the other room, if you'd like me to go get them."

"You're just younger. Can we sit?"

"Sure" we pulled out folding chairs from around my fold-out dining table and we all sat down.

"Well, I suppose my first question is how do you know what's going to happen? Does God tell you, and if so, how do you receive his message?"

She smiled at me slowly. The lines at the corners of her mouth betrayed her real age, and her nervous fingers grabbed for her necklace like it was a rosary.

"Elizabeth, I don't talk to God. I've never been introduced to the man. I just know things; I see things that haven't happened yet. Don't worry, I won't tell you about your death."

She breathed out. "Why do you only prophesize doom?"

How could I answer questions for her that I had no answers for myself? I made the cover of *Newsweek*; I saw the magazine at the supermarket before they ever sent me one. The photo they had used was one taken while I was talking. My face was contorted; the article compared me to Nostradamus, Jim Jones, Heaven's Gate. I pushed the magazine back into the rack, covering *People*, and left my groceries unpaid for in the basket. I just had to leave.

Waiting on the doorstep of my apartment was a sweet young woman and her two children. "Miss Cassandra." She stood as quickly as she could while holding a sleeping baby. A sweating, sleeping toddler lay curled, bundled up, in the stroller next to her.

"Yes?"

"I'm so glad I found you. I need to know; I need to know what I have to do. I want my kids to get to Heaven." What could I say? How could I tell this woman I don't believe in Heaven and the only Hell I have seen is on Earth? She smiled at me, trusting. She would have been happy to serve poisoned Kool-Aid to her family if only I had asked. I found myself terrified of my own power.

Perhaps *Newsweek* was right. Todd almost killed himself because of me and others will do the same.

"I was hoping you could help me. Just tell me if there is something I can do, if there is some way I can ensure their safety. Or if I can't keep them safe in this life, at least..."

"You and your children will definitely go to Heaven when the time comes. Until then, all I can tell you is love them and love life." I wondered if I were God, if I were creating this terror. Maybe, I thought, unless I accept fate, I will create it.

"Are you sure? Should I pray more, should I—"

"Just vote against Mr. White and listen to your children. Their love will be your best guide."

"That's all?" I put my arm around her shoulder to comfort her. I shouldn't—now I could not only see her future, but I could also feel it. I was her, standing in an unlit kitchen cradling a cold, blue baby, refusing to believe she was dead, kissing her soft, chilled lips, trying to breathe color back into her sunken cheeks. I started to cry, so I let go of her.

"Live and love," I said, and I walked off, back down into the subway. Once in the station the tears rolled harder, until I collapsed against the wall sobbing, unable to stop. Finally, I was numb again. I got onto the train not knowing where I was going. I knew I was never going back to my apartment; there was nothing there in my packed suitcases that I couldn't replace.

At the end of the line most everyone exited the train; the people who remained were either lost or homeless. An elderly black man, sweet smelling despite clothes that had obviously been slept in too many nights in a row, sat down next to me. The car was empty and for a minute I resented his intrusion. This was my space. I didn't want anyone, not even a homeless man, to see me cry.

"It's all right, baby, you can cry," he said to me.

"How do you know?"

"You've had a rough day, baby. It's ok. You feel like you've failed."

"I know I've failed."

"Did you do everything you could?"

"Yes, I really tried. It just doesn't seem to make any difference." I started to weep, and he handed me a clean napkin.

"So long as you tried, baby; that was all you had to do."

"But what do I do now?"

"You can choose to stop fighting."

"Admit defeat?"

"No. Make a choice, from your own free will." He got up from his seat and started for the door. "Remember, baby, God loves you." He stepped out of the subway car at 105th Street. I blew my nose and followed him out into the station. He was nowhere to be seen.

I walked out onto the street, bought a bottle of vodka and went to find an apartment to rent. With my face on the cover of magazines, I decided to change my look—long braids and a dye job. The election was only a week away and I spent that week drinking. On the bad days I would sober up enough to think. I kept thinking about Todd. Maybe Todd was still alive, 23 years old, living somewhere upstate. I should hire a detective and find out, but if he were alive he would have found me by now, thrown his arms around me and held me through the darkest nights.

I couldn't turn on the television lest I saw the news, so I watched episodes of *The Beverly Hillbillies* from morning till night. For Election Day I made sure I was sober. I had to go vote. I took only one shot of tequila. I had done everything I could, and I knew it was of no use.

* * *

I got back on the subway for the first time since I moved. I looked around for my friend, but all I saw were businessmen with briefcases and women in suits and sneakers, their heels peeking out of their purses.

I got to the polling place. The rest of the year it was just a shoe repair shop, an innocuous, barely visited location, in the basement of an old tenement building. I held the rail as I walked down the stairs. The door was open and a tiny, elderly Chinese woman smiled at me. I pointed to my name on the list.

"Please sign. Thank you."

I signed as best I could, but my hand was trembling. Another man walked out of one of the two curtained booths and gave his card to the woman. She smiled and placed it in the box.

I wondered for a minute, what if I took a gun and went to all the polling places and made them put only votes against White in the boxes—but I knew I was insane. There wasn't time, and I would be stopped. The tiny old woman smiled at me again, her eyes disappearing in a sea of smile lines.

I walked to the booth.

I pulled the curtain behind me. I wondered if this was how the condemned felt, right before execution. Standing in the little booth alone, I was surrounded by images of death and starvation.

Tears poured silently down my face, because fate hasn't changed. What is meant to be will be. I have done everything I could. The worst curse in the world was to know the future but not be able to do anything about it.

I stood there shaking, my hands frozen, my eyes crying, and did the only thing I could do, the only thing left to me. I accepted my fate; I accepted the inevitable.

Wiping my eyes on my shirt, I reached down and voted—for Mr. Leonard White.

The air was filled with a certain stillness; I couldn't hear any pained voices. The images were gone. I closed my eyes and I saw only darkness. I walked out of the voting booth, and the old woman touched my hand as she took my card. In her touch I felt only warmth and age. She smiled at me, and I smiled back.

The curse had been lifted; I could no longer see into the future.

The road ahead is dark and unknowable, and in this I find hope.

Chapter Seven

The Universes are Infinite

I came to work for the professor before Miss Felicity got sick. Once a week I would come clean up and do the heavy housework. It gave me something to do after Fred passed on. I think I was the only one in the house who even knew how to turn on their vacuum or plug in the iron. Not that the professor cared. He was happy so long as I didn't disturb any papers in the office or dust the computer.

Miss Felicity was a sweet woman. It was hard to believe that little thing could be a teacher at the university—economics or something. Teaching didn't obsess her the way physics obsessed the professor, and she didn't talk about her work much. She would come home from class and make a cup of coffee for me. Then we would sit and chat while she pulled apart Oreo cookies and dunked them in her milky coffee. Oreos were her favorite food, but she never put on a pound. Felicity had long blond hair and a pointy chin, a child's face with big eyes and a quick smile. She would ask about my family, and I would show her all the photos of my grandchildren. "You've a lovely family," she'd sigh. "You're very lucky." All of her sisters already had children. She was thirty-four and knew her time was running out.

Before the professor got married, he'd been alone in that big house. Located near the university grounds, it had been a way to recruit him to the school from his home in England.

"I was still working on my Master's. We got in the elevator together," Felicity told me. "I caught him checking me out. I looked him straight in the eye. I couldn't see his face because of his beard and glasses, but I saw his ears turning red. It was cute how embarrassed he was, so I asked him out." The professor was forty then, and a loner, but he took one look at Felicity and fell for her fragile beauty. She saw the teddy bear heart beneath his bushy beard and wrinkled suit.

"We dated for a while; then one day I moved in. I walked straight into his office while he was working on a physics experiment. I had heard that the leather chair was his favorite, so I sat down in it. He asked me what I was doing there. 'This'll be my chair' I said. His ears turned so red."

Eleven years later she still sat with her bare feet curled up under her in that big, masculine leather chair. Every night she would work there, her hair held on the top of her head with a marker pen. She would look up from the papers she was grading and smile at him, and he would smile back.

I hate to say it, but I think I noticed she was sick before the professor did. But then she was probably hiding it from him.

By the time they diagnosed her the disease was pretty well advanced, already spreading through her body. The professor called in every favor he knew. Their bedroom was transformed to a hospital, an extension of the school's Biology department. The professor would grunt at the doctors who came and went, saving his words for Felicity. They would sit in the twilight of that room holding hands and talking. "When you get better, my love," he'd say, "we'll have six kids... no, ten."

"Adam, let's start with one, unless you're volunteering to have them."

She had all the latest treatments and she fought hard, trying to live for his sake. I moved into the house to help them. The professor took a leave of absence and stayed by her side day and night, sleeping in the chair by the bed.

Visitors would come to the house to pay their respects. "It's the dean, Professor," I whispered in the professor's ear.

"I'll be back soon, Felicity." He kissed her hand as he walked out. "Bastards," he said to me. "He never gave her the time of day before, always said she was too young for me, never invited us to parties, never gave her a good seat at any dinner. They all thought we wouldn't last. I'm not going to waste a minute of the time I have left with her. Tell the dean to go away. Tell all of them to go away, Mary, or I will."

He paced the kitchen while she slept, using me as a sounding board. "This is insupportable; there must be something I can do to help her... I feel so powerless. I need to do something. There must be some way I can help her. Maybe if—"

"Now sit and eat. You don't want to get sick too."

"I should have become a surgeon... a biologist at least. I would have known. I could have seen the signs; she could have been diagnosed sooner. She could have gotten treatment earlier, before it spread—"

"What's meant to be will be, Professor." "No. I can't accept that. No. There has to be a way."

The professor started to spend his nights in the office. All night I could hear music coming from the office. He would emerge in the morning in the clothes he had worn before, his eyes sunken and dull.

Packages began to arrive from around the world; each one would disappear into his office. I asked him what they were for. "The machine," he answered but wouldn't explain further.

Miss Felicity worried about him. "Mary, he looks thinner every day. You are feeding him, right?"

"Of course, honey. He's just worried about you, is all." I brushed what hair was left away from her face. "Now let's pretty you up, and I'll go tell your husband you're ready." She smiled then, a deep and soft smile, and her eyes lit up. For a moment I caught a glimpse of the beautiful young woman she had been.

He walked in. "How is my princess?"

"Adam, you look like hell." Taking his hand, she said, "Well, we showed them all, didn't we? They said we wouldn't last, but we said till death do us part."

"Yes, but when I said that I was sure that I would die first."

"It's ok, Adam. Love is forever."

The next morning she had no smiles left. As soon as he left the room she said, "Look after him for me, please." I knew then that she had finished fighting.

She died at eight o'clock that evening, while he held her hand and I cleaned the kitchen.

I heard him call, "Mary, Mary, I need you!"

I ran into the room; her eyes were closed. He held her hand and looked up at me. "Mary... she's gone and left me."

He was weeping. I handed him a tissue.

"Can you, can you... place the calls, tell everyone... make the arrangements?" I nodded and picked up a tissue for myself. He leaned over and kissed her gently on the forehead, then put down her hand and walked towards his office. I heard him say, "The universe is infinite. This doesn't have to be."

I didn't pay too much attention; I just went to work.

Except for the funeral, the professor didn't come out of his office. I brought his meals into the office three times a day.

Before Felicity had moved into the house his office had been the living room. It was a beautiful room at the end of the house with large windows on three sides. On the left of the room was Felicity's chair and her bookshelves under the windows. On the right side of the room was another set of windows and a sofa. On the wall facing the door was the professor's desk. Sometimes the professor would be asleep on the sofa when I came in; other times he was at the desk staring at the screen. I would place his food next to the computer, and more often than not take it away uneaten. He wouldn't take any calls. I told the university that I was sure he would call them when he recovered, if he recovered.

It was about two weeks after the funeral when I walked into the office with the Windex. "That's it, Professor. I'm cleaning in here, even if I have to lift you up and clean under you."

"All right." He grimaced and went back to staring at the computer screen. The office had never been tidy but now it was a disaster, with piles of paper on every surface and overflowing waste paper baskets. Only Felicity's chair was untouched; around it was a circle of wires and electrical boxes.

Electrical wires ran from the wall to Felicity's chair. A mess of cables and metal boxes surrounded the chair. As I lifted up papers I found more computer cables ran back across the room to the professor's computer. Next to this sat large cardboard boxes, as yet unopened.

The white boards on the wall facing the door were full of red-penned equations and they continued on the windows and wall. I went to the wall and was about to spray it down and clean it off when he screamed. "No, leave that!" He jumped up and threw himself in front of me.

"Don't touch my work!"

"Professor, what are you doing?"

"The universe," he began, as if I was one of his students, "is infinite. If we track a particle we can prove that it will go along every possible path."

"You've lost me already."

"Listen, Mary, basically every thing that could possibly happen, does happen. If you throw a ball you only see the ball go from point A to point B, but we know that it travels in every direction. There are more dimensions than we can see and the ball travels through all of them. The, P-branes are—"

"Pea brains?"

"There are more universes than our own. Layers of universes upon each other, each with its own dimensions; we call them branes, membranes, parallel universes if you will. We can't see it, but in some parallel universe that ball went from point A to point C."

"Ok?" The professor had tried to explain all this to me before at some point and I hadn't gotten it then either. I saw movement in the corner of my eye and I turned. It was just Felicity's chair, empty as always.

The professor started to pace. "Each universe is on a brane; then, there is a division between each universe—"

"Like frosting between layers of cake?"

"Exactly. I just need to find a way through the frosting. Felicity is alive, somewhere. It's just a matter of finding her."

"Finding her?" God bless him, I thought, please grant him the serenity to accept his loss.

"In another universe she's alive. I've been experimenting, and the divisions between our universe and the others are not as thick as one would think. I believe that the divider is uneven, thicker in some places than others. I've seen her—"

"You need some sleep."

"Look at her chair now."

I did, and for a moment the light tricked me into seeing her face again.

"I am starting to think that's what ghosts are," he said, "just shadows from an alternate universe."

I looked around to see if there were any empty bottles. I didn't want to think he was going insane; perhaps the shock of losing her had started him drinking.

"I've turned and seen her, Mary, in her chair, bent over a paper, pushing her hair back from her face. I blinked thinking it was a trick of the light, a trick of my own grief, but she was there..."

"Professor, she's gone. We all miss her but you need to face the facts."

"Facts! The facts are she is alive somewhere, and I'm building a machine to find her."

"Ok, Professor." There was no point arguing with a crazy man. "Please shower and dress. There are clean clothes on the bed in your room."

"Thank you, Mary." He smiled at me. I looked deep in his eyes; he didn't look crazy.

It was a few days later that I found myself tripping over electrical cords all over the house. It took me ten minutes to find a plug that wasn't already in use. Then, even though I had the vacuum going, I really couldn't use it; there were just too many cords in the way.

I followed the cords into the office. Felicity's chair sat in the center of the contraption. Wires ran in a circle on the floor around it. Three large green metal boxes sat around the chair, two in front and one behind. Mirrors stood on stands in front of them. Long glass tubes hung suspended on a metal frame, swinging back and forth like those annoying bird ornaments that bob up and down. The stereo was in pieces, with three of the four speakers glued to the back of the mirrors. "What is this thing?" I asked him.

"This is the machine. The three large pieces of equipment are medical lasers." He bounded over the cable coils and pointed at the large green boxes. "The tubes are Rutherford-style particle accelerators, crude but effective. The mirrors are set in a triangulation pattern directly in front of the chair."

"What about the stereo? I thought you liked listening to music."

"Oh yes, please pick up a new stereo. The speakers I ordered haven't arrived yet but I need a vibration frequency set into the mirrors in order to create the right resonance..."

"Why do you need to use all the plugs in the house? I couldn't even vacuum."

"The amperage will short out all the fuses if I plug into the office circuit

alone, so I spread the load out through the rest of the house."

"But the cleaning. It's bad enough in here. Can't you tidy up these cords?"

"Well, we have 150 meters of electrical cable, 200 meters of audio cable, 100 meters of fiberoptic cable and 100 feet of computer cable; it won't work without it."

It all looked like cords to me. "Sir..."

"I understand your problem, Mary." He walked back to the computer and went back to work without another word. The next day an electrician came and put in a new electrical panel, and all of the cords running through the house disappeared.

I wanted him to get out, visit people, and start living again. But he rarely left his office. The machine was his life. I spent as much time as I could in the office, just to keep him company.

"Come on, Professor, you have to eat. Look, I'll eat with you." And we would sit together and eat. He would eat enough to sustain himself without ever really noticing what he was putting in his mouth. I would coax him like a child. "Come on, what would Felicity say if she saw you so thin? Come on, two more mouthfuls and you can go back to work."

It was almost a year before the machine was complete. He came out and found me in the kitchen.

"Mary?" He was excited, grinning like he hadn't since before the diagnosis. "I'm going to turn it on... I would like you there."

"All right," I said. "Do you know it's safe?""Probably. The possibilities—"

"—are infinite." I breathed in as he walked over to the machine and turned it on. It began to hum and vibrate.

"So far so good, Mary." He grinned at me again. Then he clicked the mouse. The mirrors started to vibrate. All three lasers sent streams of light towards each other. The long glass tubes tipped forward. The laser lights hit the vibrating mirrors and reflected back, meeting at a bright point above Felicity's chair. The bottom of the long tubes opened, but I saw nothing.

I let my breath out. "Is that it?"

"No, goddammit. That should have worked. Perhaps the accelerators are not producing enough gravitons..." He went back to the computer and turned the lasers off.

"What should have happened?" He ignored me, turned up the new stereo and went back to work. I walked over to the machine and looked at the mess of wires and metal. I went over to him and touched him on the shoulder but he just shrugged me off, so I left.

After a while the professor no longer told me when he was going to turn the machine on. It was just one failure after another.

The school kept the professor on the payroll, but reduced his salary because he wouldn't give any lectures. He rigged up a windmill and solar panels to power the machine. And he kept working from morning to night. The months passed, and I wondered when he would recover enough to go back to work at the university. I knew he would probably just yell or ignore me but I had to say it. "What if it doesn't work? When do you give up?"

He didn't yell. He just turned to me, his eyes filled with pain. "I can't give up. If I give up... if I say that Felicity is gone, part of my life will be gone too. All I will have left is regret for all the things I never did, all the things I never said, and then all that will remain is the certainty that I failed her."

I didn't ask again. I just made the food, kept the house and tried to keep him company.

Every time I came into the room I noticed the dust on the machine's mirrors. Yet whenever I tried to get near he would yell, and that would be it. One morning I came in with breakfast. He was sitting asleep on his computer. The stereo had been on all night but that hadn't been enough to keep him awake. I put the food down and walked over to the mirrors and started to spray them with Windex.

"Mary," he said. I turned. "Could you get me a... a coffee?" His voice was thick; he looked old. At the rate things were going he was going to join Felicity before the machine ever worked.

"Of course." I turned to walk out when I heard the machine hum. I hadn't even had a chance to clean the mirrors properly. The machine sounded different. What if I had broken it? I spun around, panicked.

The first laser beam hit the drops of Windex and turned into a rainbow. The second and third laser beams turned into rainbows too. The rainbows merged in a triangle and vibrated to the sound of the music. Then I saw the portal opening up. At the time I really didn't know what it was. I could see Felicity's chair through the rainbows, but the chair was different—the same but wrong. Then the rainbows vanished. All I saw in the center of the machine was Felicity's chair and a circle around it. But the chair was smaller, like I was seeing it through a telescope, and it shimmered like a lake. Folded on the back of her chair was a rug I had never seen before.

"Bloody 'ell, it worked!" screamed the Professor.

"Dear God," I cried.

"It finally worked... How?" he said, walking towards it, staring at her chair.

"When God closes a door he opens a window," I said, amazed.

"Not God, science. It's a portal; I should be able to travel through it. Now comes the hard part."

"It's a miracle."

"No, it's a graviton particle bridge." He looked at the mirrors and saw the drops of Windex. "Is that all it took to make it work?"

"I'm sorry. I was just trying to clean the machine."

"Don't apologize, Mary. Light frequency is important; I should have known. I'll get some prisms to maintain the light modulation. Now comes the hard part. The universes are infinite and I have to find Felicity in one of them."

We watched that other chair that day. Through the portal we could see a circle of about six feet around the chair. We could see their machine, their chair, and the viewing chairs they had set up in front of their machine. The first person we saw was an alternate professor setting up a laser and mirror behind Felicity's chair.

"Hey, it's you, Professor!" I yelled. The professor in the portal went about his business. "He can't hear me."

"The portal is a one-way door. We can see and hear them, but they can't see or hear us."

"Like the window when they do a police line-up?"

"Yes. There may even be other universes looking at us." The thought of other professors and other Marys watching us made me nervous for a while, then it went away. I suppose it was like people who are put on reality TV shows; eventually you forget the camera is there.

The professor set the computer to open the portals in each universe and look for Felicity. Even though the computer was automatic, he sat by the screen twelve to fifteen hours a day just looking for his love. "The universes seem to be arranged like a sandwich, each on top of each other. The ones the most similar to ours seem to be closest to us; by altering the frequency of the mirror resonance we can move to the next universe."

We sat together and watched other professors, other Marys watching the portals, and we watched other professors fail to make the machine work.

We looked for Felicity, and we looked for professors who had succeeded in finding Felicity. We didn't find one. As we watched their failures I lost hope, but the professor remained buoyant.

"Do you know what the odds against the machine even working were? Do you realize that in most parallel universes the light bulb hasn't been invented yet? I can wait, Mary, because we've come this far, and I know I will see her soon."

Four weeks later, the professor called me into the office. "Mary, I've found her."

I ran in. The professor sat staring at the portal. I looked. I didn't see Felicity. Then I saw her. She was sitting in her chair, grading papers. But she wasn't in the universe we were viewing; she was in a portal inside the portal. Another professor had found her. She looked so far away.

Another Mary and another professor were watching her. "Look, Mary," said the other professor in the universe we were watching. "I've been observing her, and she is well. I have to go to her."

"Wait. How do you know it's safe?" the Mary in the portal asked.

The other professor stepped towards the portal.

The other Mary stood up. "What if something goes wrong?"

"It works. It has to; the equations work," he said and walked into the portal. "Felicity," the other professor said as he walked towards his wife. Felicity smiled then stood to greet him. He reached for her. The professor put his arms out for his wife, and then he disappeared.

"Adam, where are you?" Felicity asked. "Professor," the other Mary started to scream. "Professor."

Felicity, two universes removed from us, started to scream, "Adam, Adam, where did you go?" She left our field of vision, but we could still hear her.

My professor walked over and turned the volume off. I sat watching the two portals; the professor didn't reappear in either place. He was gone without a trace. The professor started writing new equations on the board. "Could you get me a coffee?" he asked.

"A coffee? But, what are you going to do? You've got to help him," I said, pointing to the portal.

"There's nothing I can do, except work out what he did wrong and not repeat it."

"But..."

"Please get me a coffee, Mary. I've got a lot of work to do."

The experiments started the next day. The first item sacrificed to the portal was Shakespeare's Complete Works. "I am pretty sure this is the same book as the one sitting on the desk. Just watch the desk, and we will see if my theory holds."

The professor threw the book into the portal and it vanished. The book on the desk also vanished. "Hmm, ok." The professor took a piece of paper and wrote on it, and then he turned it over. "Now write anything you want on this paper."

"But..."

"Mary, the Uncertainty Principle dictates—"

"Sir, if you're not going to explain at least don't confuse me." I wrote the first three lines of *Mary had a little lamb*. The professor didn't even look at it. He could have at least told me if I had written the right thing; instead, he just folded it into a paper airplane and threw it into the abyss. It fell through and lay on the floor right in front of the second chair.

"Uh-huh. The postulate worked."

"Professor..."

He turned to me and smiled. "Mary, you've certainly been patient enough. I theorize that the reason the other professor disappeared was that two of the same object cannot occur in the same universe. I calculated that when he stepped into his portal he stepped into a universe that contained both Felicity and himself."

The professor started to draw a wave pattern on the board. "Let's say this wave is Professor A. Now Professor B exists, he has the same wave pattern but polarized differently. The two polarities cancel each other out, and both professors cease to exist—in much the same way that when an electron collides with its opposite, a positron, both are annihilated."

I nodded, still confused. "But paper?"

"The paper's exact duplicate was not in the same time and place in both universes. It was unique and thus could travel."

"Does that mean you can't go through?"

"No, Mary, it just means I can only go through into a universe that does not contain a professor."

"But how will you find one?"

"We already have." He pointed to the portal. "All I have to do is step through this portal, then step through the next portal, and I will be home with Felicity."

I shook my head at the sheer craziness of the idea. "Professor, you don't even know if you will survive the first portal, let alone two of them. Just because the paper airplane didn't explode doesn't mean you won't. I mean, you could end up with your insides out, or your outsides in."

"Or with the head of a fly?" He smiled.

"Exactly, just like that movie." I was too upset to notice he was laughing at me.

"We will do some more tests, Mary. I don't want to die, I don't have faith in an afterlife, but I know that in this life Felicity is still alive. All I have to do is reach her."

* * *

So we adopted pets—lab mice from the Biology department, an old deaf monkey, and a lame dog. We sent the mice through first.

The professor dropped a trail of food all the way to the portal and the mice followed it. They seemed to just step from our universe to the next without noticing, still looking for the next piece of food. "I need to call the exterminator," said the other Mary when she saw the mice. She tried to hit them with a broom. The mice all seemed alive and well on that side. At least they ran fast enough while escaping her.

The dog was sent through with a note on his collar. The professor threw a ball, and he chased it through. The other Mary came into the room after he had arrived. She took the note off, read it, and then the other Mary started to talk to us. "It's so strange. Your note says that I am watching me. It is all too confusing. I'll push the dog through for you. He seems well and fine, so I may as well do it now. "

Mary put the note down, and then pushed the dog through with a broom, staying well away from the portal. She'd seen the professor disappear and she wasn't about to risk it herself. The dog appeared in Felicity's universe unharmed.

Felicity found him later in the day. "Where did you come from, boy?" She bent down and cuddled him. "Maybe you can keep me company until they find Adam."

"I don't even know why I haven't just gone," he growled. "The dog was fine. Felicity is waiting for me."

"You can't afford a mistake. Please test it again. For me," I said. "You know I'm going to miss you."

The monkey was next. He had become my pet and he didn't want to go. He fought to get out of the professor's arms and come back to me. "Hide, Mary. So he can't see you." The professor put his hand over the monkey's eyes while I hid behind the curtains on the end of the room. "Look, monkey, there's Mary." He pointed to the other Mary inside the portal. "Go to her. She's waiting." The professor pushed him gently and the monkey walked through the portal to the other Mary. I came out of hiding to watch. The monkey arrived on the other side. Then he climbed into the other Mary's arms and started to scream.

"Calm down, baby," the other Mary said to the monkey. He flung himself about and she put him down on the floor. He went into a seizure and started to shake. We watched as foam came from his mouth. Then my little monkey was still.

"Dear God!" I started to cry.

The other Mary put her head to his chest. She tried opening his eyes. She put her hand in front of his mouth. She picked up the poor dead creature. "He's dead." She started to cry.

"He's dead. We killed him!" I yelled.

"Professor," said the other Mary, "I don't know what happened. I think the shock killed him. Maybe the smarter you are the harder it is on you?"

The professor just sat down and began to scribble notes again. Then I heard Felicity's voice. She was sitting in her chair crying.

"Adam," she said, "where did you go? The police can't find you, I've been looking for you everywhere, but you just vanished. I can't sleep. I can't eat. I feel like a part of me has died. The last place I saw you was here. I hope it wasn't your ghost telling me you were dead. Adam, it's been two weeks. I don't want to live without you. I love you. Come back to me."

The professor got out of his chair and ran for the portal.

I ran towards him. "No, don't!"

The other Mary screamed as he materialized in her room. He fell forwards, tripping over the dead monkey. The professor lay still on the floor.

"Professor!" I screamed, sure he was dead.

The professor stood up. He kissed the other Mary on the cheek. "I'm fine, look."

"But the monkey..."

"The damn monkey was old and sick." He looked directly back at me. "Mary, there are two wills in my desk, both leaving the house to you. Send one over here." Then he kissed the other me on the cheek and stepped through the next portal and straight into the waiting arms of his wife.

"Felicity.""Adam! Where have you been?" They began to kiss, and we all cried.

It's been a year now. Both portals are still open. Sometimes I send the other me a note. Sometimes she just sits and talks to me. We watch the professor and Felicity, and the lame dog; they've called him Pete. Felicity is expecting their first child, a girl; they want to call her Mary. We keep the houses clean and ready, because you never know what might happen. The universes are infinite and anything is possible.

Chapter Eight
Letters Home

J ared walked into the tent carefully, pulling the layers of doors closed behind him. The heavy lead one first, then the plastic shield they said would keep out the gas, then the khaki camouflage fabric one that reminded them where they were. He kicked the ice off his boots, then slowly, like a man much older, he pulled off his protective helmet, and removed the gas mask. Carefully he climbed out of the bulky radiation suit and hung it on its hook. Stripped down to his fatigues, he opened the next layers of tenting and walked into the warmth of the mess hall.

He walked over to one of the computers lining the walls and logged in. "Sergeant Jared Light," he typed quickly. Clicking the mail button he held his breath; it seemed to take longer every time. Four new emails. He opened the folder. It contained an offer for a new mortgage, two new porn ads, and one of yet another pill which if purchased would make you into a sex god. Nothing from Sara. It was probably too early. He'd only sent his email 4 hours before as he went on patrol. He wished she'd answered; he just wanted to hear from her. They had never been apart this long before.

Sara sat at her computer and read Jared's email. *He is missing me. He loves me. What to say? Stevie—now there's a safe subject. Stevie almost never mentions Daddy. He is just going on with his life the way a five-year-old could.* **Hi, Honey,** she typed. **Stevie lost his first tooth today; the one at the bottom front, at the left. I'll send you a photo later. He is very proud of himself. He put it under his pillow and is waiting for the tooth fairy tonight.** *...Better not tell him that I spent $20 on a present for Stevie to celebrate. He probably thinks that a quarter under the pillow is enough.* **He was very brave, didn't cry or anything. He wanted to show it to you.** *...One of the few times Stevie wanted his daddy. Usually he is just happy to have Mommy all to himself.* They spent each night snuggled up together. Jared would never have allowed that, but Sara loved having her son close to her. That warm, undemanding tenderness made her want to cry when she realized how big he was getting and how soon it would be before Stevie wouldn't let her cuddle him anymore.

I got new sheets and cover for the bed. It's a great cranberry red color with little ties all over it. *...Better not dwell on that, or he'll want to know how much I spent. It's my money too. I bring home a paycheck too. There's always plenty of money for his latest toy, but if I want to buy something for Stevie or me...* **I'd like you home and naked on the new sheets. It's been so long.** *...Even before you left it had been too long. Where did the passion go? Is it because of Stevie, or the other pregnancies, or is this just what happens after 10 years together?* **I miss you so much...** *when I think about you, which is less and less. Sometimes I forget I'm married and I can't picture your face.* **When do you think you'll be home? Write me back as soon as you can. Love, Sara.**

Jared checked the computer again when he hit the barracks. There was an email from Sara. His eyes devoured it *...Stevie has lost a tooth already?* **Dearest Sara, WOW! Stevie lost a tooth! It seems only weeks ago he was born. Don't know when I can get home. There are no leaves. Counting the days till my tour's over.** *...If I survive 'till then. It's still 5 months and men are dying out here every day. They canceled the leaves 'cause they can't get enough new recruits to kill.* **Of course, it could be over soon and I'd be home.** *...I used to believe that. I used to think we could win quickly. Now I don't think anyone wins. I just want to go home.* **The weather's colder now.** *...If the enemy doesn't get me, the ice will. Billy lost his nose last week. His wife'll never kiss him the same again.* **I miss sitting in front of the fire cuddling you. Can't wait to get back home to you.** *...If I get* *out of here alive. We lost 12 men from this morning's patrol. If I get home I will hold you every night until there's no strength left in my arms.* **Would love if you could send me another pair of socks; they were great.** ...*Ok, they weren't great, but they keep me from getting frostbite, and I use them for gloves to sleep in.* **Soon, as winter gets here, they'll be really useful.** ...*I can't believe this is only fall. The natives live underground. We bomb their little dugout houses looking for terrorists and guerrillas. What is the difference between a native and a terrorist?* **How's Stevie doing at the new school? Does he have friends?** ...*Last night I shot a boy Stevie's age. How can I tell you I shot a baby 'cause I thought he was carrying a gun?* **The new bedspread sounds great. I'd luv to be wrapped in it now. I'd kiss your toes then work my way up till u screamed into the new pillowcases and then back to your toes to tease.** ...*God, I'm so tired I feel nothing.* **Need to sleep, love. Hope to dream about you all night, dream I'm undressing you, dream I'm home. Night, Jared.**

Jared was awakened by the sound of incoming fire. He stumbled in the darkness to put on his boots but fell to the ground as a shell hit the barracks. The room exploded into clarity of black and burning white. Jared ran toward his protective gear, forcing himself to breathe slowly, quietly trying not to inhale the radioactive dust from the shell fragments.

Sara opened her email as soon as she awoke. She smiled as she saw there was another from Jared.

"Mommy!"

She turned to Stevie.

"I need juice."

"Ok." She wouldn't get any peace until he had what he wanted. Giving him his juice, she walked over to the TV. Some kick-boxing cartoon was on and he sat two feet in front of it. She sighed thinking if she were a better mother she would make him go outside and play but knew at least now she would have some time to write Jared and tell him what was on her mind.

Dear Jared,

I went out to the movies last night. My mom babysat. *...Something she wouldn't do if you were here. She'd say that my husband should spend more time with the child and make me hire someone if I wanted to go out with you.* **I saw a new movie, *Locus Night*; you'd like it.** *....And the male lead was gorgeous. Oh my God, the bluest eyes I've ever seen. If I met him in real life and he wanted me I'd so cheat on you.* **If you get a chance to watch it you'd enjoy it.** *...I think you'd enjoy it, not that you'd want to pay money to see it in the theater. You always think that's a waste of money.* **If you don't get to see it while you're away I'll rent it and we can watch it together.** *....I may just rent it and watch it again and again. Oh damn, it's been so long. I just want to be fucked. Everywhere I look I see gorgeous men.* **Stevie is doing fine at the new school. He's invited to his first birthday party this weekend. I'm sure he will have fun.** *...Of course he'll have fun. Without his daddy watching him he'll eat sugar till he's sick. And I'll eat sugar too. I may as well get some pleasure out of this life. You are going to tell me I'm fat when you get home but you should be happy. If I start losing weight, that just means I'm shopping for a new man.* **We are going to have a Halloween party at work next week so Stevie and I are going out to look for a costume. Stevie wants to dress like a solider.** *...or a pirate, or a robot, but Jared should at least think the kid wants to be like him.* **I'll email you photos when we finally get him all costumed up.** *....Oh damn, how do I put this...* **And it's no pressure but I really think I want to have another kid. I know it hasn't worked out that way yet, but I don't want to give up on the idea just yet. I**

just feel like if I don't have a daughter I will regret it my whole life. *....Should I have written that? Oh, Jesus, I can't keep everything a secret, can I? I want another kid. Despite the miscarriages, I still want to try. Oh please, God.* **So get your butt back here safe so I can molest it, ok?**

Love, Sara.

His men surrounded Jared, dressing in silence. They strapped on their guns and went out into the field. The enemy were gone, disappeared back into their burrows, and an air strike was already underway targeting the area the shells had come from.

Jared gathered his men, and they stripped down their fatigues and entered the line at the infirmary. They'd been there enough times; they knew the drill. Each of them took a saliva stick. If the stick turned blue they'd be staying for more tests, otherwise they'd just take a urine cup and bring back a sample of urine tomorrow morning, then donate yet more blood to the cause.

With the stick in his mouth, wanting something to think about for the minute until he could remove it, he walked over to one of the computer stations in the waiting area and logged in.

Dear Jared,

I went out to the movies last night. My mom babysat. *...She wouldn't babysit if I was there. That woman has always hated me.* **I saw a new movie, *Locus Night*; you'd like it. If you get a chance to watch it you'd enjoy it.** *I'd love to see a movie. I want to do anything but this. How much longer do I have to have this thing in my mouth?* **If you don't get to see it while you're away I'll rent it and we can watch it together. Stevie is doing fine at the new school. He was invited to his first birthday party this weekend. I'm sure he will have fun. We are going to have a Halloween party**

at work next week so Stevie and I are going out to look for a costume. Stevie wants to dress like a solider. *...Do the solider costumes come complete with radiation detectors and breathing masks these days?* I'll email you photos when we finally get him all costumed up. And it's no pressure but I really think I want to have another kid. I know it hasn't worked out that way yet, but I don't want to give up on the idea just yet. I just feel like if I don't have a daughter I will regret it my whole life. *...I want you to be happy. Haven't I always done whatever I could to make you happy?* So get your butt back here safe so I can molest it, ok?

Love, Sara.

He took the tester stick out of his mouth slowly—blue; he'd known it would be. He and five of his men joined the line.

* * * * *

They brought a laptop over to his bed. The machines were running beside him, cleaning his blood. The worst of the cases had been shipped to the hospital, but he was still there, on the front lines.

Hi Sara,

Sorry I didnt answer fast; I'm in the infirmary. There's not much wrong. Got a few days off to rest. *...If only I'd swallowed a couple more rads I'd be on my way home right now. Now they'll just send me out again.* **Johnny n Fred might look u up. U remember them; they were discharged last week and I told them to come see u.** *...Maybe they can tell you what it's like here. Maybe they'll tell you all the things I can't write 'cause the censors would erase them, tell you all the things I'll never be able to say 'cause I'll scream.* **They r running some tests on me now—probably nothing. Odds r Ill be back to work in 2 days.** *...Back to killing little kids and chasing ghosts we never find.* **Tell**

Stevie when I was his age I dressed up as a ghost. I'd luv to see him dressed up as a ghost or a monster, or a pirate, or something. *...Not a solider. God, not a solider. I don't want my kid following in my footsteps. You can't really want him to grow up like me, Sara, grow up never seeing his family, dying in a war known only by the year it is fought 'cause there's nothing else unique about it.* As for another baby, u know I'd luv another kid. I thought we agreed not to try more but it's your body if you want to. Please don't put too much stress on it. If it happens it happens. Gd willing, I'll do my part. *...The last two miscarriages almost destroyed us, Sara. You haven't been the same since the first one. I feel like you don't want me anymore. You only want sex for the baby, and if I don't knock you up then it's such a frantic panic, with no passion or love, only fear of failure.* Ill email you soon. Luv Jared.

Dear Jared,

Are you ok? Are you out of the infirmary? *...What's wrong? You didn't tell me what's wrong. Why didn't you tell me?* Your friend Frank rang this morning and came over to see us. I remember when he was in high school with us. *...I had a crush on him back then, but you asked me out first.* I barely recognized him. He's so grown up. *...So old and shattered. Will you come home like that, Jared?* He told me about the barracks. He told me what happened. Are you ok? He thought you were. He said he'd gotten too much exposure so they'd sent him home early. *...How could you volunteer for a war like this? Depleted uranium shells used by both sides poisoning the air.* Please be careful. *...Don't come home like him, tired and old, poisoned by ammunition, dying slowly.* Tell me what's wrong. I'm worried about you.

Sara

My dearest Sara,

Theyre sending me home. I've had enough. *...Enough depleted uranium, progressively building up in my organs, the radiation leaching into my bones, that I'm finally going to be able to leave.* I'll see u soon. Ive missed u both so much. Tell Stevie that his daddy's coming home.

I luv u. Ill let u know when Im arriving.

Luv, Jared.

Jared,

You're coming home! *...Don't come home sick. Don't come home sick. I don't want a sick man.* Oh my goodness, what a surprise. When do you expect to be discharged? Maybe we could make a sister for Stevie sooner than I thought. *...Or maybe that's why he doesn't have a sister already. Have you been sick for a long time now? Maybe it wasn't my fault we couldn't have a kid. Maybe it's your fault. You shouldn't have joined up. What if we have a deformed kid like Mary? What kind of man is coming home? Are you going to be like Frank, an invalid, a cripple who will suck my life from me?* Then again, maybe we should wait a while, make sure you are healthy. I can't wait to have you home again. Sara.

Sara my darling,

Theyll send me home via Edmunds Air Force base. I'll have to spend a couple of weeks be4 they send me home. *...I want to be walking before I come home. The treatments are killing me, Sara. I feel so weak. The guy in the bed next to me says they can't cure the radiation poisoning yet; they are just experimenting on us. They want to know if there is a way to start treating all the bystanders of the wars.* Ill ring u when I get stateside.

Luv, Jared.

Jared,

Are you ok? *...I know you're not ok. You must have been exposed when the shell hit the barracks. How dare you get sick! I always thought you'd come home dead or alive. I was prepared for that, but not for half-dead.* **How are you doing?** *...And I'll be stuck with you for the rest of your life. I can't leave a sick man. How could you do this to me?* **I'll wait by the phone until you call.** *...My life's on hold until you're dead. I wish I was young again. I don't think I love you anymore. I don't know that I ever did. Where is that great passion, the one that survives everything? I should be happy you are coming home. Instead I want to hear you are dead so I can start again. Maybe I missed my true love and settled for you instead.* **Call as soon as you can. Sara.**

Darling Sara,

Spend tomorrow by the phone, have the new sheets on the bed. *I'll do my best to make love to you, to make you happy.* **I missed u so much.**

LuvJared.

Dear Jared,

Stevie is waiting for you. *...I had to show him the photos to remind him what his daddy looked like. We were so young in the wedding photos. I've been with you all my life. I don't know what my life would be without you in it. I don't know if I am in love with you but I love you.* **I'm so happy you're coming home.** *...Maybe we can start again. Maybe we can find the passion. Maybe it's enough that you love me and I am used to having you around.* **See you soon, dear. Love, Sara.**

Jared walked slowly to the pay phone in the airport. He was pale and weak, but the pain had subsided, and he was almost home. All that mattered to him was that he was home, and he was alive; that Sara and Stevie loved him, and were waiting for him.

Charity

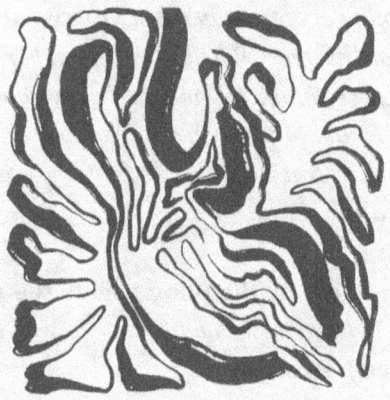

CHARITY
/CHerədē/ noun

The act of giving to those you have deemed less
worthy thatn yourself. Also the businesses that profit
from the things given by donators without expecting
payback.

Chapter Nine

Gifts from the Gods

I t was when Junie asked me if I'd met her sister Margaret that I knew she had the same holes in her memory I had. Of course I hadn't met her sister. Her sister lived in a different city to either of us. I'd never even been to the city her sister lived in and her sister had never been to mine. If she had remembered why we knew each other she'd know that. I thought, perhaps it was selective memory, perhaps she didn't want to remember why we knew each other or how we'd met, perhaps she didn't want to remember the details regarding how we became friends.

Sometimes I worried about how much I couldn't remember. Sometimes I walked into a room with something in my hand and not only did I not know why I'd walked into the room but I couldn't remember what I had in my hand. I'd have to look down to see it, and there it would be, the groceries I had to put away in the cupboard, the school T-shirt I had to put in my daughter's drawer.

"Oh, don't worry about it," Susan said as she poured herself another coffee from behind the coffee shop counter, then walked down back to her chair as a customer to sit back down. "I haven't been able to remember anything since I got pregnant with Olivia and she's eleven now." I nodded and got back to work. What was I doing again? I put some of it down to stress and not getting enough sleep. It was hard to sleep when you were a new mom, let alone when you were running a business.

But that was five years ago, and in some ways it was better and in others it was worse. It was like I no longer remembered that I'd forgotten. There was nothing there at all, and the holes weren't obvious to me. At least until someone challenged me for information.

"Mom, what was my first word?"

"I don't know." How was it that I didn't' know this? I knew it was important to me, I knew it mattered, I knew I'd known this once. "Honey, did you have lunch yet?" *Lunch. He wants to go to lunch with me. It's 1 p.m. Did I have lunch? If I did what did I eat? Am I hungry? I'll say I haven't had lunch. I want to go to lunch with him. If I've already eaten I won't eat much.* "No." "Ok," he said, and I wrote down on my hand where he wanted me to meet him for lunch because I didn't want to forget. I didn't want to get in the car and not know where I was driving either. I didn't want to get in the car and do that automatic thing where I just drove back to work or home because these were the two places I drove to.

I tried not to worry about it. I mentioned it to my doctor at my regular check-up. "Is there a family history of early onset Alzheimer's or dementia?"

"No." Not that I could remember. Well, my mother was losing her marbles but no one had ever diagnosed her with anything. Maybe soon, but not yet, not before she's 70 at least, because she'd have to get a lot more frail before one of us could drag her to the doctor.

"No diagnosis of Alzheimer's in the family?"

"No." Not yet.

"Then I wouldn't be too overly concerned. If you feel it's getting worse I could make a referral to someone." A referral. I looked around his office covered in posters from drug companies. For this kind of hideous fungus use this cream, for birth control use this implant, for genital herpes here's a pill. I wished my problem was so simple. Not "I think I'm losing my mind and I'm so scared I don't know what to do," but "Oh, Doc, I have a blister. Is there something you can do for it?" A referral from him would take months to get an appointment with an HMO guy who'd tell me there was nothing wrong with me. I'd try for the appointment with the neurologist. As long as I didn't have to pay for it, I'd wait. In the meantime I'd try to get more sleep.

Although Junie didn't remember why I'd never met her sister, I did. I'd never met her because Margaret'd never come to the wedding of my brother and Junie. In fact, I didn't go to it either. It was one of those Vegas things best forgotten and annulled. Junie and I stayed friends because my brother had forced us to live together long enough that we'd grown to like each other. I guessed Junie was just blocking most of the memories of the brief ill-conceived marriage to my brother, but who knew? "No, Junie, I've never met Margaret."

"That's right. I couldn't remember."

"Do you find yourself forgetting more things since your kids were born?"

"Yeah, sort of. I remember being a child perfectly, then at about eleven I start losing things. I figure I just started throwing things out so I can fit more in."

My mom's always said the same kind of thing. When she lost my birth bracelet for three years when I was a child all she could say was, "I don't know where I put it." Of course, like any precocious and obnoxious child, I'd respond with "But you must know." And she'd reply, "I can't keep everything in my head, you know. I just sweep out all the useless information." Now I had to wonder if she wasn't right. Although I'd researched it on the internet, it seemed like there should be no limit to what the brain could hold. Perhaps there were scientists that knew more than me. Perhaps all the information was there and I just couldn't get to it.

And I had to wonder who I really was. Wasn't I just a collection of memories? A history of events that only I knew? And if I had no memories, was I nothing? I started writing and journalling in a desperate attempt to retain pieces of myself, of my memories, of who I thought I was.

Without my memories, were pieces of me gone forever? Would I be a different person if I could remember more, or remember differently?

* * *

The neurologist stared at his monitor. It looked like the subject was suffering anxiety. Scared about her memory loss, questioning her own sense of self. There was nothing else for it. She was too young. Knowing wouldn't help much, and he wasn't sure; the results were inconclusive.

"Well, everything looks fine. We'll schedule you for a check-up appointment in six months. For now, don't worry. Stress can lead to memory loss as much as anything."

"But I'm afraid."

"Yes, we'll give you some pills for the anxiety." *She's probably losing her mind and there's nothing I can do to stop it. At least this way she won't have to worry about it too much. Next visit I'll see if there's more scarring in her brain, then I'll tell her. For now, well, she shouldn't think about it too much.*

* * *

Two hundred years earlier his grandfathers had been sent to help the mission and today was going to be his first day working for the cause. He understood how important it was. If he didn't succeed his entire species would die out.

"Thomas," the Suit said, walking in. It was the CEO of General Motors and he didn't feel the need to address him formerly; he was just a chemist. "I understand you have solved the engine knocking problem."

"Yes," said Thomas. "We have added lead to the gasoline; tetraethyllead, to be exact."

"But the reports I had said you were working on tellurium. I mean, tellurium is toxic but no one knows what it is. But everyone knows what lead is and that it's poisonous." The Suit stiffened. "This won't work at all."

Thomas turned on his motor, then poured some of his formula in. The sound of the motor went from banging to purring. "We can call it ethyl, sir. It will make the engines much more efficient."

"My," said the CEO, walking over to touch the engine that was now purring along. "Yes, we will call it ethyl."

* * *

"Tom, sit down. You look awful." His wife pointed to a chair.

He fell into the chair. "Can you bring me aspirin and water?"

"Sure, honey. How did it go today?"

"They want to close down the plant just because of the deaths."

"Won't the high heat system make it safer?" she said, putting the pills next to him and the water in his trembling hand. "No one will die making ethyl soon. And I couldn't let them close down production so at the press conference I poured it on my hands and breathed it in for a while. I told them it was safe."

"Did they believe you?" She walked over to the stereophone to put on his favorite album.

"Yes, it worked. Ethyl will stay in production. They won't be able to keep the planes in the air without it." He put down the glass and started unlacing his shoes. She reached down to help him, pulling them off and putting on his house slippers. "And the new cloroflurocarbon project is well underway. I have also given them a catalyst to crack hydrocarbons.""That's good, dear." She brought him over his dinner on a tray and placed it in his lap. "It's the refrigerant that will eat the ozone layer, right?""Yes. You know, if they had just made these humans a little smarter they wouldn't have had to send our mission to speed up the process.""Yes, well, your granddad and dad did the best they could making the saw blade that would aid defoliation and the tire that would enable road travel, but you've done more for the cause than anyone. And I am afraid it's killing you."

"I know it is, Carrie, but at least when I die I can go home. It's you I worry about, and the kids. They'll be growing up on this planet in these short-lived bodies and the lead will make them and everyone else less intelligent. Little Tommy probably already has enough lead in his system that he won't be able to be an inventor like the rest of his family.""He's a happy little boy; he will be ok. You're doing all the heavy lifting. By the time the chlorofluorocarbons are in place there won't be anything left on the mission orders."

He reached out his hand to her. "I love you.""And I love you." She smiled down and sat in the armchair next to him. "The kids will be all right. We can just bring them up as normal little kids. They don't need the burden of the mission that was passed down to us."

"Yes, you are probably right. They don't need the cultural memories. They don't need to yearn for a world they will never know.""Lack of memory is the best thing we can give them," said Thomas. "They don't need the burden."

   *   *   *

20,000 years before

"Do you think they'll ever work it out?" said the neurologist.

The politician looked down at the fetuses in the tubes. "Not if you've done your work."

The reporter clicked pictures and pulled out her recording device. "So, for the record, how does this work exactly?"

"Well," said the politician, "we're seeding the planet with a slave subspecies. They will tame the vegetation and plant life and make the planet fit for our arrival."

"And what's to stop them evolving and fighting us off when we arrive like the colonists of E-45?" E-45 would be in her headline; it would make better press that way.

"Would you like to answer this one?" the politician pointed to the neurologist. If anything went wrong, he wanted the neurologist to take the flack.

"I have genetically altered the stock. Not only are they better suited to a high-oxygen atmosphere but they are very short lived."

"How short?"

"Instead of 2000 years they live less than a hundred."

"A hundred?! They'll only be children."

"Yes, and that should stop them from developing normally. They will have no cultural memory. Every generation will have to learn everything from the beginning. In addition, if any of them question their lives too much, it will overload the synapses and their short-term memory facilities will begin to shut down."

"Why do we want that?"

The politician was going to take the credit for this one. "Well, it's so when we come to take over they won't have developed the weapons to fight us, of course. They'll be too busy in their little short lives, and if any of them start trying to think about why it should be so, they'll be incapacitated. We are planning to colonize in about 20,000 years. By then we calculate they will have started using the fossil fuels and adding enough carbon to the atmosphere for it to be acceptable to our people. Then we'll be able to take our colonists who are hiding in the asteroid belt out of stasis and send them down."

"Wow," said the reporter with a toothy grin. "You heard it here live on News TV. Back to you, Rick." She turned the camera off and started to pack up. She looked momentarily at the little jelly-like babies growing in the sterile goo. Poor bastards. At least they wouldn't remember how badly life sucked.

Chapter Ten

Hark the Herald Angel Sings

I t's almost Christmas again. It's been a year. And yet when I walk through the store I see the toys I would have bought him for his first Christmas, the little onesies, and tears leak out. Tears leak out a lot. I pretend they don't. The first time I wrote this story I just went through everything as it happened. You had to follow along with me, and learn that my grandson died like I did, slowly at the end, hoping he was fine until you lost hope and fell into the despair. When I first wrote this story I wanted you to suffer. Now I don't. Now I want to let you know, going in, that this isn't a feel-good story of hope and redemption and you can stop listening now. You have been warned.

You would think by now we would have all the answers. It's 2080, for God's sake. AI advances have fixed lots of problems. There are no more traffic fatalities, no more pollution problems, carbon sequestration is advanced enough that we don't have a lot of the worries that plagued my parents, and yet babies still die before they are born. Yet we don't use those words—DEATH, BABY. Instead we change the language as if it diminishes the pain. It's not a baby, it's a fetus. It's not death, it's a miscarriage, or stillborn, or fetal loss. A miscarriage, like you took a chicken out of the freezer, carried it wrong, and dropped it. Or stillborn, as if the child is born like a doll, all perfect and frozen in a smile. Or my favorite, fetal loss. You were on your way to being a mom and somewhere along the way the baby was just misplaced, like your phone or your purse. Later you'll find it.

And the numbers haven't really changed over the years. A certain amount of pregnancies are lost. I lost two myself, but we don't talk about that. Women don't talk about our issues. We just keep going. Female issues are best ignored where they can just disappear like a festering boil. At 90, my grandmother kept counting the birthdays of the child who should have come after my mother. He would have been 53 today, she told me the day she died. He would have been 53. I have managed to forget the birthdates of my two miscarriages. It's easier that way, easier to focus on the children I had, easier to endure. Like the hot flashes and mood swings, cramps and childbirth, being a woman is about pain. It always was. Men don't even begin to understand how much easier their lives are, and we don't tell them. We endure.

Of course, the real reason we don't communicate is because no one wants to listen. You tell someone you had an accident and everyone leans in and asks what happened. You tell them you lost your baby and they sit back and go quiet, at best they say "Oh, my," then ask about the weather on Tuesday. So you don't say anything. It's not anything anyone wants to hear. And for that reason I am now probably talking to myself. You probably tuned out five minutes ago. And yet I still need to say it.

I like to think that things will change, that in the future babies who are wanted and loved won't die before they are born. I'd like to think that women should have a choice and those who chose to have a child can. I'd like to think we'd spend the money on healthcare to make sure every baby loved and wanted was born, that we'd do the research. But we don't. We spend more money extending grandpa's forgetful and painful life by six months than we do making sure that his great-grandson can exist. I think in part it's because we don't talk about it.

Over a century of arguing about *Roe v. Wade;* you would think we would care about babies people want. Ok, I need to get off the soapbox. This is a story about a woman's right to choose, but it's not about abortion. Abortion you already care about, one way or the other. Miscarriages and stillbirth, premature babies dying before they can live, these are things no one but the family cares about. Everyone knows a pregnancy should be 40 weeks; that's full term. Everyone knows you can't have an abortion after 15 weeks, because the government has decided you're killing your child. Everyone knows that 24 weeks is when a fetus is just barely viable. At 24 weeks the baby goes in an incubator and most of them make it out alive—most of them, but not all, not even now. We know so many things but we don't know how they feel.

Like most bad news, it started with a phone call.

"It's too early," his voice tore from the phone.

"It's too early." I heard the words rip from my throat, repeating him, for there was nothing else to say.

"I am on my way to the hospital. It will take me 40 minutes to get there"

"I'm leaving now too. I am probably more like 60 away in this traffic." Rush hour. Why did it have to be rush hour? I threw myself in the car, wiping my tears on my sleeve. I had already set the directions for the hospital into the GPS. I was due there tomorrow with her for an ultrasound. Tomorrow, the 19th December, I was going to get off work early and go with her for her 24-week ultrasound. Just routine. Her hubby would be working and it would be my first chance to see my grandson, to see Gabriel. I pressed the button to drive.

It's too early. That was my only thought. This wasn't the plan. How early was it? Definitely not the 40 weeks that was normal, not even thirty. It was too early. We'd just found out weeks earlier he was a boy. A little boy, my first grandson, Gabriel, a person already in the minds of his parents. A child conceived in love and hope, a boy who had already played outside and been called back in his mother's dreams. Gabriel, a good solid name, a name that would work for a boy and a man, and now he was coming. Too early.

Later I wouldn't remember the drive. Later I wouldn't re-member wiping my eyes and nose on my sleeve till it was soaked. In the moment it seemed to take forever to get there. I put my foot down as hard as I could on my old car. If a cop wanted to give me a ticket for turning off the auto-driver and speeding, he would have to follow me all the way to the hospital to write it; I wasn't stopping.

My son-in-law was standing in the parking lot when I drove in. He waved his arms and I parked beside him. "They won't let us into the building until our lab work is finished. I started mine. Go to the security door." I walked up slowly, moving through the air as if time had stopped and I was having to fight the inertia of the universe. Security noticed my approach but did not speak until I was close.

"State the purpose of your visit," the door screen in the center of the door said in a neutral, accent-less, emotionless, perfect, mechanical voice.

"My daughter is in labor."

"Her name."

"Susan Merters... Augustino." I almost forgot she had changed her name. She wasn't my daughter anymore, she was his wife. I needed to remember that. I was invited only under suffrage if I behaved. She wasn't my little baby anymore and I couldn't hold her and make it all better. That man, the one standing in the parking lot already, the one I often thought wasn't worthy of my beautiful, intelligent baby—he was the one she had called. He was the husband. I was only the mother-in-law, the butt of jokes and the one who was tolerated, mostly.

I understood my role. But my baby was up there in that building somewhere, in pain, and all I wanted to do was get to her and hold her hand. And tell her the pain would pass. That she was stronger than the pain, stronger than she knew.

Tell her the wisdom that sounds like a platitude, that things would get better.

"Insert your hand in the reader," said the door, and a portal opened with a hand scanner I placed my hand on. The sensors were already scanning my body even if I couldn't feel it, sensing my temperature, cardiac rhythm. A small prick pierced my skin and I knew they would test my blood for any infectious agent. Since the pandemic you couldn't enter unless you'd been tested. It would only take a few endless minutes. Then they would know everything—my identity, my vaccination status, my marital status (single since four years after Susan was born; terminally single. I would die of loneliness; I was sure they knew that too), my cholesterol and whether I was carrying anything that would spread to others.

I walked back to Angel, my son-in-law. He was sitting on his car hood, tears streaming. It struck me how I had never seen him cry. My tears were gone now. Now I needed to be useful.

"They said I was overdue for a booster, and they won't let me in till it's had a half hour to work in my system," he explained, gagging on his own grief.

"We will probably go in together then," I said, having the question I had not yet asked answered. Why my baby was alone. Why in the end, after all the planning and preparing, she was experiencing the worst thing in her life alone, with only strangers.

"Gabriel is 24 weeks, isn't he?" I said. "The 24-week scan is tomorrow, right?""Yeah," said Angel. "But he's still 16 weeks short... I mean...""Yeah." Twenty-four weeks was so premature. "Maybe they can stop the labor. Another two weeks even would make all the difference."

Angel nodded. His watch buzzed and he wiped his face on his sleeve. "I've been cleared to enter. I will see you there."He walked off, straightening himself as he neared the door, bracing for whatever came.

My wrist buzzed and I walked up to the door again. It swung open when it read my ID signal.

The floor had a blue-lit path and I followed it to an elevator and then up and up. It opened and I followed the lights out to the labor room. Susan sat upright, cradled in Angel's arms. She was white, tiny and worn out, and I was glad he was there for her.

"Hi, baby."

"Hi, Momma."

Angel answered the questions I didn't want to ask. "She delivered Gabriel while we were in the parking lot. They took him straight to the NICU. Susan didn't get a chance to see him, or touch him. The doctor is supposed to be coming in a minute to tell us more.

I sat down on the other side of Susan and took her hand. "Oh baby, I wish I had been here sooner.""Yeah.""The labor was fast," I said, knowing I was babbling, needing to fill the silence.

"Yeah, but it was more painful than I could imagine.""I did tell you.""There are no words that can describe it."

"Yeah."

Angel was stroking her hair. "Did they tell you anything before they took him?"

"No, but I heard him cry before they took him. That's a good sign, right?""Yeah."The doctor came in without knocking. He stared at his screen as if that were the patient and then spat the words out hurriedly as if that would make it easier to hear. "I am so sorry, Susan, you son was born dead."

"But he wasn't dead." She started to sob.

"We measured him. He was 23 weeks 6 days and had not reached the 24-week viability mark. So, his organs will be used to help others."

"He's dead?""Yes, but his life is already helping others as his organs are being harvested right now."

"Gabriel's dead? He can't be dead. I heard him cry.""I will leave you with your family to grieve."

He shut the door as he went out, but he would have heard the scream Angel let out even with the door closed.

I looked over at my tiny, devastated daughter doing her best to comfort her broken husband and I knew I was not wanted. I told them I would be outside, but I don't know if they heard me, and I went outside to cry alone, in the hallway, under the Christmas decorations, while my brave little baby cried for her dead son.

Chapter Eleven

Last Plane Leaving London

T he plane was supposed to leave at seven. We'd boarded on time, the normal rush of people waiting to stand in line. I sat. No point in standing before they called my group boarding number. I had booked my seat deliberately in the rear of the plane, in July, when I had planned this vacation. It was the cheap seats, and there was never any overhead luggage space left but I didn't care.

I had an aisle seat and I was close to the bathroom which, as I got older, seemed like a better and better idea. And somewhere, always in the back of my mind, was the thought that if something goes wrong, your survival rate is better in the back of the plane. A passing thought, with images of old-fashioned jumbo jets smashed into mountains, or broken and burning on the tarmac, fleeting through my consciousness. I didn't want to admit I was superstitious, but I had been booking the rear aisle seat on the right-hand side of the plane for 35 years now. And, so far, I had always arrived alive.

I looked out the windows. In Heathrow, the snow was still falling, gentle wind swirling the white puffs. I'd seen worse. Driven through worse in Utah, white-out blind, trying to follow the snowplow while the fury of angry mountains blew across the highway. They were boarding group B. I would be up soon. I wondered if Sara and Dave had finished packing yet. Not that they could take much in two backpacks. I hoped the woolen socks I had left would be useful.

They called my group and I stood slowly, not rushing to stand in the line. There was time. There were six people on the standby list sitting near the gate, their faces more and more dejected. It looked like everyone had shown up. The gate attendant called a name and a middle-aged man rose eagerly and ran to the desk as fast as 30 years' sitting behind a desk would allow.

"Yes, I'm Underwood. You have a seat for us?"

The us was his wife, a thin, pale American Gothic of a woman, sitting quietly, with too much carry-on luggage. "No, we've space for you, sir. One seat."

"Can she go instead?"

The words were barely out before she ran up to the podium, leaving all the luggage behind despite the repeated warnings about not leaving your luggage unattended. "No, Sam, you go."

He ignored her. "You must have another seat. We've been waiting on standby for two days. She needs to go. Don't you have another seat?"

"No, sir. One of you can take this flight and one can wait for the next flight."

"Then she goes." She started to cluck but he ignored her with the practice of years. "Iris Elizabeth Underwood. She gets the seat. I will wait for the next flight."

"She" was voicing her distress but the gate attendant ignored her too. He was the one who made the decisions. That was obvious. The gate attendant printed the boarding pass, and he took it and walked back to the seat, leaving her to trail behind him.

"Sam, I don't want to go without you."

"I know, but it will be fine. I will catch the next flight out. The kids need you home and I will be there soon."

"Ok, sure, you will be home soon after me." His voice got louder as he lied, hers got quieter.

"Group five," a faceless voice called.

The young man in shorts behind me decided to start a conversation with the young man next to him, speaking too loudly, of course. "I was here on vacation. How about you?"

"Same, man, just enjoying the pub scene."

"Yeah, the beer was warm, man." That seemed like a dangerously ironic thing to say now.

"Yeah." The young man in shorts tried to steer the conversation into safer territory. "I'm from Long Beach. Where are you going home to, man?"

"Indio."

"Cool. Nice ATV trails out that way."

I walked away. I couldn't stand their loud, energetic voices. It was all too much. I put my hands on the glass, looking out on the runway. Cold, I held them there, uncomfortable but real. The cold was honest, painful and intense, and removed from the mindless noise of my fellow countrymen, all escaping and making their way home. The night was falling; the gray day was turning into a black night.

Time to board. I entered the gate last and had to wait for the young men comparing their tattoos and stories of hangovers to clear the ramp before I could actually board the plane. I swerved around people still playing with their luggage to make my way to the back. Iris Elizabeth Underwood was in the center seat, that single open standby seat, and a beautiful young woman sat by the window, her headphones on, her phone in hand.

We'd been on the tarmac for an hour by the time they pulled away from the gate. Snow was still falling, light and airy. You could still smell the deicing chemicals on the inside of the plane. Normally if a plane was late people would be complaining but no one was saying anything. Like at a funeral or in a library, everyone was either silent or spoke in hushed whispers. A few people had gotten up quietly to use the bathroom. Even the arrogant young men had run out of words. I had been trying to read my book. Trying not to think about Sara, but unable to help myself. I had tried texting her, but she hadn't responded. Too busy, I guessed, or out of range. Dave was a sensible guy. She would be all right.

Until they met two years ago, I wouldn't have guessed Sara would get married. I suppose I always saw her as my free spirit unfettered by conventionality. But then she was also malleable, my child who wanted to please, wanted to be loved. And Dave did love her, unconditionally. I knew that when he told her to go home with me—not that I could have gotten her a ticket, but the fact that he was willing to be alone was a sign of love.

We were all just sitting there with tray tables and chairs in the upright position. The stewardesses were buckled in, waiting, and then I heard the pilot speak and I knew we'd be leaving. I hadn't been sure till then. Hadn't been sure that we wouldn't be sent back to the gate, back to the airport, back to Sara. I almost hoped the plane wouldn't leave, that I could go back to Sara. It didn't seem right that she was staying and I was leaving.

"Flight attendants, sit down for departure," barked the pilot. He had an accent; French-Canadian, I guessed, and used to snow. He sounded desperate. We pulled out slowly, the engine revving at high speed, the noise unlike anything I'd ever heard before.

The high-pitched cry of the engines belied how slow we were moving, bouncing down the runway over mounds of ice and snow, screaming turbo jets spinning in place while we slid and skidded down the runway. And then the pilot let off the brakes and we shot forward, up a snow mound and into the air, the engines still screaming in the frozen air.

I wondered if Sara and Dave had made it to the Chunnel yet. The exodus had started two days earlier, but they had stayed in London till my flight time. "Sara, I can give you my ticket." Dave had tried to get her to take it. We both loved her more than we loved ourselves. It's lovely when your daughter finds someone who puts their needs after hers. "You're young, darling. You should go."

Sara looked at Dave, her love unquestionable. "I want to be with Dave. You need to go back. Amie's kids need their grandma home. You can't stay here; they need you. And Mom, you are right. I am young. I can walk. We'll be fine."

The TV was on, showing pictures of the refugees, their kids in wheelbarrows and strollers. Young kids on their parents' shoulders, old people supporting each other. The entire Chunnel full, wall-to-wall humanity leaving as quickly as they could with all they could carry, before the food ran out, before the water froze and broke the pipes, before the gas lines burst.

"We're both young and strong, Mom. We'll walk to Marseilles. They are running refugee ships across to Morocco. It will be warm enough there. We'll find work. We'll be ok. I hear the US government might even send planes for US refugees."

She believed what she said but I didn't know. Dave dug his car out and drove me to the airport. Sara sat in the backseat with my carry-on. I wished she was still small enough to sit on my knee. Who was this beautiful woman who had replaced my baby girl? I kissed her goodbye and while Dave was getting my suitcase out, I gave him my wedding and engagement ring and my diamond earrings and all the money I had been able to get out of the ATM before it stopped. I shoved it all in his hands. "Look after her."

He nodded and put everything in his pocket.

They'd been walking for at least five hours now. I wondered how far they had gotten.

The plane bounced on the currents and we climbed slowly out of the city. Below, the center of the city was black. I guessed the ice had taken out the power lines. I didn't know if I was relieved that we'd gotten off the ground.

As my eyes turned from the window I caught Iris's face.

"We were on our 25th wedding anniversary trip when the Gulf Stream stopped." She pulled out a tissue and blew her nose, her eyes still dripping.

"I was visiting my daughter," I said, and she handed me a tissue.

Chapter Twelve

Donations

"No, no," my mother screamed. "What about grandchildren? I was going to be a grandmother." As if my being gay was all about her, as if I had gone out of my way to ruin her plans and future life. At twenty, I'd never thought about my mother wanting grandchildren. She was only 42 at that point and liked to dress like she was an eighteen-year-old cheerleader. The idea that she wanted grandchildren hadn't occurred to me. And it wasn't going to change anything anyway. I handed her a tissue and she wiped off some of the makeup that surrounded her green eyes. She still looked good at 42. Auburn hair and green eyes was unusual enough that she would have gotten attention from men without wearing the miniskirts, but what do I know?

"This isn't about you. I am gay. You must have known." I'd rehearsed everything I was going to say and she wasn't following the script.

"I thought you'd at least get married and give me grandkids. Have a boyfriend on the side. That's how it was always done. Why can't you do that?""So you think it would be better for me to live a life that was a lie?""Why not? It's not like the rest of us live the lives we want. You think when I stand all day at an open house telling people about the benefits of having six bathrooms it's the truth? You think that I tell my co-workers that I come home every day to this ratty two-bedroom apartment because your dad stole the house in the divorce?" She waved her arm around, highlighting the rental beige walls and beige carpets and gray tiles and gray tile countertops. It wasn't that she hadn't tried. The walls were hung with art and the window sills were sparkling with crystals, but it was admittedly an ugly box with poor lighting and small aluminum windows. But it was rent-controlled and she paid the rent for both of us. She'd paid everything my whole life and now she wanted something from me and I couldn't deliver. "Do you think I tell people I think my son is gay? Life is a lie! After all I've done for you all I wanted was a grandbaby or two to hold and hug. Was that so much to ask? Hasn't my life been hard enough?"

I shook my head and started packing my things. I moved into my car parked at the 24-hour Fitness on 31st Street, and a few weeks after I left she found a boyfriend with a house with six bathrooms, four bedrooms, an ocean view and six grandchildren. So I had done the best thing I could do for her, moving out.

When I had moved from our rent-controlled apartment in Santa Monica my dream was to move to the village of WeHo Rainbow, one of the many gated enclaves of the city. Although I'd grown up on the Westside, I'd grown up on the beach tourist/hippie district. I hadn't traveled anywhere else. Being as it was the tourist area, I had met people from all over the world, and the rest of the city would travel to us. They would ride the Ferris wheel, walk on the concrete boardwalk on the beach. The beach was neutral territory so everyone was welcome who wanted to spend $93 on a cheeseburger and $120 to park for the day. You needed papers to go to other parts of the city. The village of WeHo Rainbow had been walled in since the terrorist attacks in the 20's. I would need to pass a psych eval and physical to enter, and it all cost money. They weren't going to let any more people in who'd been wired to explode at a nightclub. The Hills was mostly a DMZ. You could go to Rodeo Drive to shop with a guard or two, and the residents had their own walls and guards. I'd been there a few times but didn't really see the point, because I couldn't afford a designer fanny pack or electronic tattoo. The largest area that was threatening to encroach on the rest was the West Side Ervu. While population growth in the other areas had stopped and was declining, the Orthodox Jews were still popping out

10-15 kids per couple. They'd been one of the first areas to wall themselves in. With it they created a boundary that let them move about on the Sabbath. I understood why they'd built the walls; the bombings had made them scared enough to build their own Jewish Ghetto. The rest of the city, everything east, is greater MexiCal, and not being Latinx I haven't been there, just seen it on TV.

This year Josue, my boyfriend, offered to take me for Day of the Dead to visit his family and all his ancestors, but I was too scared to go. I thought that as a red-haired, green-eyed, 6'4" guy I would stand out. He told me his family would love me no matter what, and I am considering it Christmas. He brought back amazing food and I am wondering if it's worth getting travel papers to go. He says that MexiCal is very accepting of all kinds. I find that hard to believe from what I see in the news but he swears it's true.

I think the conflict between WeHo and the West Side Ervu was a basic one of different beliefs. Here's these people trying to live a conservative life where they don't watch TV, don't go on the internet, don't let women expose their knees or elbows, and here's the Pride parade going past their house in a neon thong. I don't know if I would have got the job I have right now if I hadn't gotten it using my Beach paperwork. But then they were desperate for employees.

My mom was probably right. Not about everything, mind you, but about staying in school and getting a degree. My argument was a degree in what? With AI taking most of the jobs over the last couple of years, it wasn't like I was going to be an accountant or a copywriter. Hell, even most of the actors have been replaced by dead versions of famous people. Monroe's image in various states of undress must have done at least five movies last year, and that's if you don't count the porn ones.

So getting a job has been hard. When I first moved out I was living in my van. And anyone who tells you how fun that is has never tried to stay clean by buying a gym membership and washing their socks in the sink while sweat pours down their butt crack. I parked at a park during the day for a while. It was fun, got to watch all the single young men bringing their dogs for a stroll, but I knew it just wasn't my place anymore. There's this special something when you feel at home, and I had never felt it before I moved to the WeHo. I always felt like everyone was looking at me and I was some kind of freak, which apparently I was. So there's that, but being a tall, thin man with auburn hair and light green eyes is much less of an asset in a straight society. I knew I had to get some money and apply for travel papers to go to WeHo.

And I was desperate for money so I answered an ad I saw on a holographic billboard on a park seat. "Sperm donors wanted. Top money paid." It was just down by the old airport. I could park on the runway that night and walk over. The office when I arrived was smaller than I expected, but how much real estate do you really need to pay rent on when you are only asking men to come and go?

The girl at the desk was beautiful, part of the enticement for the heteronormative men who came, I am sure. She was also surprisingly nice in a city where beautiful women tend to be rather vain and rude. "Can I get you a coffee while you are filling out the paperwork?" she asked. The forms asked for my address, and the state of my sneakers probably told her the truth of that.

"Yes, please," I said. And she brought coffee, cream, sugar, and a plate of cookies, which I gratefully accepted. The forms were long.

"This is the worst part," she said. "Unless you are afraid of needles?""Needles?" How the hell were they planning to take the sperm?

"Yes. We need to take a blood and saliva test for DNA and communicable diseases.""Oh yeah. No problem," I said. Not like I'd been able to afford a physical in a while. They could at least tell me if I needed to see a doc. The forms wanted to know about my parents, about their parents, about their jobs and diseases. They even wanted to know if there were any religious affiliations so I wrote how my mom had been born Jewish but only practiced to the degree that she gave lousy little presents for Chanukah instead of getting me some decent gifts and a tree like all my friends seemed to have. Then there was an IQ test. By the time I'd gotten through all of it I felt like I deserved more than just a plate of cookies and a good coffee.

Celia, the girl who was even nicer to me as she'd realized I wasn't interested in her, showed me through to the office, touching me lightly on the elbow. She was one of those girls who saw men who didn't hit on her as a challenge rather than gay. The lab tech in the next room collected my papers. He was quite beautiful too. They obviously paid well and deliberately hired based on attractiveness. He took a cheek swab and drew some blood. Then he looked over all the papers. "I've got to make sure they are complete," he said. "Your eyes aren't contact lenses, are they?"

"No, and the hair isn't dyed. The drapes match the carpet too," I said, checking him out.

"That will be popular." He smiled and reached out, touching my hair. "Yes, it's a very unusual color." He pulled back. "We will reach out tomorrow, after the test results are in, to let you know if you are qualified to donate.""Oh," I said, looking down at my totally falling apart sneakers. "I was hoping to get paid today.""Celia will give you $400 for coming in today and completing the induction."Four hundred dollars! It wouldn't pay the rent but I would be able to get a hamburger and some new kicks. It felt like Heaven. I had been so scared I would have to go on my knees back to my mom's house and beg her new boyfriend to let me move into the basement and stay out of the way while my mom pretended to be a twenty-year-old debutante. I really didn't want to ruin her fun and rain on her parade. She had worked her ass off all those years to keep me fed and housed and in nice clothes. I needed to be able to make it on my own, and $400 would be a nice start. I was feeling cocky so I said, "Well, if all the tests come back negative or positive in the right way, would you have dinner with me tomorrow?"

He smiled on one side, and I knew when I came the next day I'd best be wearing clothes neat enough to go out to dinner afterwards.

The worst thing about being on the streets is the nights. They are so long, and I would lie on my back seat curled, with my knees up around my ears, listening to the sounds of the city. It was better in a car. Most of the unhomed, as they like to casually refer to the 50% of the population of Santa Monica district who can't even afford an ugly, falling-down, rent-controlled apartment, live in tents. In a car you feel safe; there are doors to lock. It takes some effort for someone on a bender to break your windows, rape or kill you. In a tent or wrapped in a sleeping bag, it's best to catch all sleep during daylight hours and spend the nights walking or sitting up, watching for the dangers. I could never get comfortable, yet I would catch sleep in starts, waking to the sound of coyotes coming out of the hills to eat garbage, and rats, or the sound of meth addicts dancing and screaming at the voices in their heads.

When I woke, there would always be some part of my body that I had never really noticed before asleep and in pain. The amount of pain that can come from the back of the knee or the sixth rib right at the side is something I really hadn't appreciated. I had almost $200, a new pair of shoes and a full stomach, and I slept worse than normal, terrified that someone would have noticed my new kicks and tonight would be the night they would break the window of my ancient Tesla 3 and kill me for the cash in my pocket and a pair of shoes that were probably the wrong size for them. I couldn't sleep at all so I drove to the beach. The recyclers were going through all the trash cans looking for anything of value to recycle and sell. One looked over at me, his body wrapped in layers of beach towels and cast-off sweaters, and he looked straight in my eyes. In his face I saw hate and fear. He was afraid I was there to rob him, and his fear was a palpable weapon of destruction. So I drove away to the edge of the city. The wall of the Ghetto had been a wire line once. Now it was 12 feet tall and extended through the city, across the hill, to the valley. It was the second largest Ghetto after the one built in Brooklyn. They say the one in Brooklyn has a population of about 6 million, and the one here is getting close so I guess Hitler didn't win after all, even if he did manage to reduce their population by a third. My mom's great-great-grandfather was killed in a camp, and her great-grandmother was a miserable bitch who narrowly escaped death only so she could psychologically torture her children. Ok, I don't actually remember her. I am only quoting my great-grandma, who would tell me Bible stories when I was a child. She was about 100 then, so I have to give her some leeway, but I am not sure telling eight-year-old kids stories about men who would have killed their beloved son to please an invisible deity if a bush hadn't caught fire and told him, "Oh yeah, sorry, that was just me testing you, ha ha, my bad," is really appropriate. I drove down the wall of the Ghetto. The apartment buildings within kept growing higher every year. And the guard towers were all manned.

Next I drove to the walls of WeHo Rainbow. They were covered in rainbow paintings and razor wire. I'd only seen pictures but I knew I wanted to live there. I wanted to be with my people. This donation could pay my way in. The sun was rising in the east in a dirty orange haze, so I caught an hour's sleep at a parking meter on Santa Monica Blvd, then woke back up with a new crick in my neck. Sleep was impossible. I was excited to be able to start my life. So I ended up driving to the clinic early with a drive-through coffee and a tube of nutritional goo in my hand, and I waited till they opened.

Celia walked up to the door and I followed her up. She heard me behind her and I watched her shoulders tense, then she turned and looked at me. "Oh, good morning, Joshua. Welcome." She waved me in and I walked in, grateful to be able to sit inside with air conditioning while she turned on all the lights and got ready for the day. "Your tests should be ready by now. Let me just fire up the computer and get them."I sat and found I could not relax. My foot was wiggling and I realized that I was nervous. Maybe my genetics was broken, maybe I was the carrier of some disease I didn't know I had, or worse yet, maybe there was some disease like early onset Alzheimer's that I was just about to find out I had. The seconds became hours as I contemplated the myriad of ways I could die alone in my car of some horrible condition I never knew I had.

"Well, Joshua." Here it comes, I thought. "You are a perfect donor. No problems at all, so we are good to go."

The air I didn't know I was holding released. Everything was good, and I would make sure dinner tonight was good too. My life was about to begin.

"Would you like a cup of coffee before you begin? Maybe a muffin?"Oh hell, yes. A morning that started with a coffee, a muffin and masturbation. Life really didn't get any better than this.

A half hour later I was in a small room with a screen and my choice of pornography. The banana nut muffin had been my best breakfast in a while, and I thought it was the best ironic choice for the job ahead. It was harder than I thought it would be, just because it mattered for once. I thought about all the thousands of stained sheets that had been wasted over the years.

That evening, $2500 richer than before I had gone to donate, I took Bruce, the lab tech, out to dinner at the pier. The evening cost me $500 but it was more or less worth it. After everything I had spent and needing to eat, I had the $1500 needed to apply for the travel documents. I went and got fingerprinted, and sent in all the forms with the application form. And it was going to be four weeks before I heard back.

Bruce was nice enough to let me stay a few days, but he wanted love and I was not even ready for a four-week commitment. I had $17 dollars left and a new pair of shoes. I wasn't worth the price of a cherry slurpy on the open market. I needed some more cash. So I started looking for sperm banks. Turns out you can only really donate twice a week, so I was making sure that every other day I was hitting a different bank and not doing anything fun in between. Still, four weeks in and I had over $10,000 saved up. That would be enough for first and last on a studio apartment in WeHo; at least I hoped it would. I started applying for jobs. I mean, at some point the donations would need to stop. I was hoping to spend my sexual energy doing something much more fun.

I applied for every damn job going and mostly I was rejected by the AIs within hours of applying. "Thank you for your interest in working for..." It was at the point I didn't even remember all the jobs I'd actually applied for so it was no great loss when I got yet another rejection letter.

I was scanning through my email deleting junk when I saw, "Thank you for your interest in working for..." and I was just about to delete it when I saw the next line. "Interviews will be held Monday at..." An in-person interview. Who the hell did that anymore? I looked down. It was a job inside the eCRV, inside the Ghetto. I had to apply in person at an office near the beach, and if I passed the interview and background checks, I would be working behind the walls.

Wow. I had never thought I would see behind the walls. The idea of seeing where all those people lived was almost as exciting as the idea of getting a job at all.

The man behind the interviewer desk looked normal, no long side curls by his face. I wanted to ask but I kept biting my tongue. "The job we are hiring for is security guard.""For the wall?""No, those jobs are only for people of the community. This is a guard job at a local school inside." He had a generic face. The only thing I was sure was that he was straight."If they have the guards on the wall, why do they have them for the schools too?""There have been incidents. Nothing major. I mean your life won't be in danger, but... Well, there have been threats and the school wants to make sure that their children are safe."

"So what would I need to do exactly?""Well, you'd greet the kids and let them into the school, then stand outside the gates making sure no one else gets in during the day. Then at the end of the day you would supervise them crossing the road and going home.""So I'd be a crossing guard?""Yes, sort of. Most of the children walk to school and live nearby. You may also have to help children get in and out of their cars."What he didn't tell me was that the kids who came by car were usually getting in and out of limousines. There were public schools within the neighborhood, and the extra cost to send your child to a private school was not for the middle class.

Of course, I don't know if he could have really explained it to me. I mean, I'd seen the guys with full-on hairdos and black hats and coats on a summer's day talking business at the beach, and I thought I understood their lives from the exposé TV documentaries that regularly came out, but nothing could have prepared me for the five-year-old boys already in school away from their sisters, playing soccer with their little yarmulkes and prayer shawls. No matter how much they slid in for the goal, their little hats stuck into their short, spikey little haircuts while their side curls were baby hair-fine, flying about as they wrestled and threw each other to the ground. I would stand on the outside of the fence to the soccer field and watch them for hours. Whenever a toy came flying through the fence, usually because one kid was trying to torture the other, they'd say, "Hey, Mr. Joshua, could you throw us back our toy?" You got to feel kind of protective of the kids. I kind of felt like all the kids were mine. And I wanted all of them to be kept safe.

Their moms would drop them in the morning, with their double and triple strollers and their perfect hair. Perfect because it wasn't their hair at all. They probably had no hair left, but the wigs were all straight, lovely hair, straight from India or somewhere else, highlighted and styled to the latest fashion. The moms would drop the boys at the one school, the girls at the other, then walk the babies and toddlers back home. In general they seemed like good moms. I never heard one yell at a kid. They were calmer with six children in tow than my mom had ever been with one. I supposed if you've got one kid you worry. If you have a half dozen or more you just can't be bothered stressing. I'd never seen so many kids. I kind of wished I'd grown up in the Ghetto with 12 siblings, because how could you be lonely if you were never alone? Growing up with just my mom I was usually alone and I had never thought about how that shaped me till now.

Friday afternoon school closed early and I would head home, through the walls of the Ghetto, before they closed for Sabbath. It was a good job, and I was happy to have it. I was also happy to have my one-bedroom apartment in the WeHo with Julio, and my life was as good as it had ever been. Even my mom and I were in a good place, and she'd invited both Julio and me to Thanksgiving dinner with her newest boyfriend.

The table was set with enough food for twenty, which was twice as many people as had been invited. My mom was feeling magnanimous. She'd just sold an ocean-front house in Malibu, so her commission would keep her fed for the next year, and Paul, the latest boyfriend sitting down at the far end of the table, was genuinely in love with her by the way he smiled at her.

In the five years since I'd left she hadn't introduced me to most of her boyfriends. I think because she didn't want most of them to realize she was older than she looked. And because she was still ashamed of me. But I'd managed to keep a job for almost five years, I'd been with Julio for two years, and I think she was actually proud of me—not that she'd say anything.

"You know, Joshua, now that you're in a stable relationship maybe you should look at having a kid," she said.

"A kid?""Yes. I have some money saved up and I could help pay for a surrogate. Use your DNA, get a donated egg—""You've thought about this.""Yes," she said. "You were such a beautiful baby with those bright green eyes and those fine red curls. I always wanted to be a grandma and you would make such beautiful babies. All the people with money are getting test-tube babies now. I mean it's just safer. With all the genetic diseases, it's better to know."

Adelaide, my mother's best friend for 30 years—although for reasons no one but my mother could understand—piped in. "You know, when I started working at the doctor's office twenty years ago, all these Jewish couples would have to come in to see if they were carriers for Tay Sachs. You know, the families were all so inbred after the Holocaust that they had a lot of genetic diseases. And Tay Sachs was the worst. You have a beautiful little baby and by the time it's five it's dead. In the end a lot of them had to use donor sperm or eggs." Julio turned to Adelaide, hoping to distract my mother and save me. "Oh, what kind of doctor do you work for?" "I work for a reproductive medicine doctor. I could introduce you. Dawn has been talking about it for a while and I can help you guys out."

My mom stared at Adelaide for saying too much. "Obviously the decision is yours, but it's just that you would make the most beautiful babies, Joshua."

I started to cough and Julio stepped in to save me. "He certainly is beautiful, isn't he? That is a very generous offer. We will need to discuss it."

"Yes," said my mom. "Of course." Although you could see from the look on her face that she hadn't really thought that Julio would have any say in it at all. She wanted a little red-haired grandchild whom she could mold into all the things her son had never been, someone who wouldn't disappoint her. Suddenly I was mad at her. All my buttons had been pushed and I was ready to scream. It was at this point that Paul stood up.

"I would like to thank you all for coming today. I asked Dawn already and she said yes, so I would like to announce it to all of you, our friends and family." He nodded at me. "This beautiful woman has agreed to become my wife."I looked around quickly. The house must be worth at least 100 million, and the research I'd done on him said he was a widower with no children and a company on the stock market that was worth several trillion. So that was why my mom had offered. She knew she could afford whatever it cost, and now that money was no object, the one thing she wanted was a grandbaby. It was a wonder she wasn't just planning on popping one out somehow herself. A kid who wouldn't be a disappointment.

"Congratulations," said Julio, raising his glass, and the rest of the party followed suit.

Monday I considered not going to work. Mom was rich now. If she wanted a grandkid she could pay. I wouldn't have to work again. But I found myself getting up and getting dressed. It wasn't because I had to; it was because I really wanted to go, to see the kids. Julio and I had discussed it all weekend. We both liked kids. We both had thought it was impossible. But his family would be happy for him to become a dad. Except in the Orthodox Jewish culture, kids were a status because they were so rare. When I was out of the Ghetto I saw maybe 2-3 kids a month, less in WeHo.

I was a few minutes late and the strollers were lined up to drop off the kids. A young baby started to cry and the mom bent down and grabbed up the rotund little redhead infant. The baby flashed its green eyes at me and I realized my mom was right; I had been a cute baby, and this baby looked like me as an infant. And so did the toddler with the mom behind, and three five-year-old boys who looked like brothers but weren't, different yarmulkes pushed into their spiky red hair.

And the older boy with the red curls coming down the sides of his face walking his red-haired sister to the school next door, and I didn't know how I hadn't seen it before. See the light green eyes, so much like mine, and combinations of red and auburn hair. Jews had been using donated sperm for years to get around genetic defects. These were my kids. I had been the donor. I started to laugh.

My mother already had hundreds, maybe thousands of grandchildren.

About the Author

I grew up watching the *Twilight Zone* and *Star Trek* and reading Isaac Asimov, Frederick Pohl, Cordwainer Smith, Phillip K. Dick and Octavia Butler. If that wasn't enough to distort my sense of reality reading "Examination Day" by Henry Slesar when I was 12 was probably the nail in the coffin.

I love stories about normal people who find themselves in unexpected situations, whether that is because the world just ended, or because they have just moved to a new planet. I like to explore human limitations even while the human in question no longer has a body or was never human to start with.

I believe that Speculative Fiction has been one of the driving forces of this modern era making us reach for the next great advance. And yes, I am still waiting for my flying car, so to all you guys with better science skills than me, please hurry it up. Stories can make us think of all the possibilities and consider what future we want to build.

I always enjoy a story that surprises me and tests my view of reality. I hope you do too and will appreciate my offerings to the gods of speculation. – S.A.Wooderson

Also By

Other books in the Future Sins and Virtues Series include:

Future Sins Volume One

Future Sins Volume One features the first four of our basic sins: Greed, Envy, Wrath and Sloth. For we have not overcome our basic flaws as humans but carried them on into our future. Greed, the most virtuous of all modern sins, will drive men forward towards the next invention, the next frontier, for what they can find and exploit. For those who do not have the gifts given to the few, there is always envy. Envy is the subtle sin, that lets a teacher hate her students, even when they are destined to save the world. These stories range from a world where we can communicate with animals, to one where children are owned by the rich. Wrath, the rage of the righteous, or the insane; both equally valid in a future where vengeance is scientifically enhanced. A Sloth slowly shares its evils over both volumes.

Future Sins Volume Two

Future Sins Volume Two crawls out of the gate with two tales of Sloth, one in which belief and science battle for the soul of a young man and the future of humanity and another where a different young man discovers a secret hidden in plain sight. Lust is the next of our sins, the possibilities of love and sex in different alternate realties. And Gluttony is a desire that is hard to satisfy, whether it is seeking something new and untried or just trying to mine the most minerals possible. Meanwhile Pride comes before a fall and Jacob Levin is about to find out the hard way how deep the hole he has dug is. Meanwhile pride is going to rise Una high, up above the earth and all the people who pity her. The last story of this collection is The Elevator's Arrogance wherein Bob the elevator repair man is back out trying to save the world, one elevator at a time.

Other works by S.A. Wooderson:

Children of the After Life – Currently on Kindle Vella and coming out soon on Kindle and Paperback

A dystopian novel of the survivors of a global pandemic. The flu pandemic has been spreading for ten years, killing off everyone but the young. The government has taken the healthy to live in small enclaves while the cities are run by armed gangs trafficking in anti-viral medications. Sara barely remembers what life was like before. She spends her energy trying to navigate protecting her younger sister and surviving. She's one of the few people who have never gotten ill and the government wants to find out why.

Nothing To Be Afraid Of – Coming out March 15, 2024 on Kindle and Paperback

This collection of horror short stories lies in the space between reality and insanity. Are these stories about people who have briefly touched evil, or just stories of people who have lost their way? These are stories about ordinary people and the fears that come for us all.